GOOD-BYE[illegible]

So what if Tanya's a [illegible] Carole said to herself [illegible] the younger girl bring the bridle's crown piece up over Starlight's ears, being careful not to catch his forelock under the browband. *So what if she doesn't always seem to listen to what I'm saying? She's probably just excited. She definitely seems to like Starlight so far. And I'm sure she'll like him even more once she puts him through his paces.*

When Starlight was ready, Tanya swung into the saddle, not even waiting for Carole to give her a leg up.

See? Carole told herself. *Tanya's a terrific rider. Starlight is really responding to her. Does it matter if she seems . . . well, maybe just a little too sure of herself? He wouldn't let her get away with it if she didn't actually know what she was doing in the saddle. And that's really all that matters, right?*

**Don't miss any of the excitement
at PINE HOLLOW,
where friends come first:**

#1 *The Long Ride*
#2 *The Trail Home*
#3 *Reining In*
#4 *Changing Leads*
#5 *Conformation Faults*
#6 *Shying at Trouble*
#7 *Penalty Points*
#8 *Course of Action*
#9 *Riding to Win*

And coming in March 2000:

#10 *Ground Training*

PINE HOLLOW™

RIDING TO WIN

BY BONNIE BRYANT

BANTAM BOOKS
NEW YORK • TORONTO • LONDON • SYDNEY • AUCKLAND

Special thanks to Sir "B" Farms and Laura and Vinny Marino

RL 5.0, ages 12 and up

RIDING TO WIN
A Bantam Book / December 1999

"Pine Hollow" is a trademark of Bonnie Bryant Hiller.

ISBN 0-553-49287-X

Published simultaneously in the United States and Canada.

Bantam Books are published by Bantam Books, a division of Random
House, Inc. Its trademark, consisting of the words "Bantam Books" and
the portrayal of a rooster, is Registered in U.S. Patent and Trademark
Office and in other countries. Marca Registrada. Bantam Books, 1540
Broadway, New York, New York 10036.

PRINTED IN THE UNITED STATES OF AMERICA

OPM   0 9 8 7 6 5 4 3 2 1

My special thanks to Catherine Hapka for her help in the writing of this book.

ONE

"Whew!" Lisa Atwood exclaimed, rushing into Pine Hollow Stables with her head ducked down against the pouring rain outside. As she pushed back the hood of her raincoat and shook out her shoulder-length blond hair, she spotted Carole Hanson, one of her best friends, pushing an empty wheelbarrow down the stable aisle. "It's coming down like cats and dogs out there," Lisa told her.

Carole smiled a hello, then glanced at the door, looking worried. "I know," she said. "This rain came out of nowhere, didn't it? Max had us turn out a bunch of horses in the big hilly meadow this morning because we all thought it was supposed to be nice."

Lisa shrugged off her dripping raincoat. As she headed across the entryway toward the student locker room, she paused long enough to peek through the partially open wooden door of Pine Hollow's indoor schooling ring. "Where's Stevie?

I thought she'd be here, practicing for the horse show," she commented. "I only see Callie."

"Callie got here a little while ago for her therapeutic riding session." Carole pushed the wheelbarrow against the wall and stretched. "After the crazy amount of work I've been doing around here lately, I think I could use one of those myself."

"Not me," Lisa said. "I could never work as hard as Callie does." Their friend Callie Forester had lost partial use of her right leg in an automobile accident a few months earlier, soon after her family had moved to Willow Creek, Virginia. She was doing her best to regain the full use of her body through physical therapy, particularly therapeutic riding. At first it had been a slow process. But lately, Lisa could see Callie getting stronger every day.

"Good point." Carole stretched again, then reached to tighten the band holding her curly black hair in its thick braid. "She's barely missed a day since she started. It's no wonder she was such a great endurance rider back in her old hometown. She's got endurance coming out of her ears."

"And it's no wonder her doctors are amazed with her progress," Lisa added. She ducked into the locker room long enough to hang her raincoat on one of the row of hooks inside the door.

"Last I heard, she was hoping to get rid of her crutches by Christmas—maybe sooner. Stevie has even started taking bets on when it will happen."

Carole glanced around with a slight frown. "Speaking of Stevie, where is she?"

Lisa laughed. "I asked you that same question about two seconds ago, remember?" She and Carole had been friends since junior high, along with their other best friend, Stevie Lake. So Lisa had long since learned that when it came to horses—or her part-time job at Pine Hollow—Carole never had any trouble focusing. When the topic was about anything else, however, she could be a little scatterbrained.

"Oh. Well, I don't think she's shown up here yet today," Carole said, "which is weird, since the horse show is less than a week away. The rest of us have been putting in every second of practice time we can manage."

Carole and Stevie were among the five riders chosen by Max Regnery, the owner of Pine Hollow, to represent the stable at the Colesford Horse Show, which was being held in a nearby town. The riders had been training intensively for more than a month.

Lisa tilted her head to one side and squeezed some rainwater out of her hair. "It's hard to believe it's so soon; it seems as though Max only just announced it."

Carole nodded and glanced at her watch. "Five days, nineteen hours, and oh, around twelve minutes," she said. "But who's counting?"

Lisa smiled. "Don't worry. Even if the show were in five minutes instead of five and a half days, you know you and Samson would be ready."

"Thanks." Carole's answering smile was grateful but still a little anxious. "But I'm glad it's not in five minutes, because I have a ton of work to do before I can even think about tacking up Samson for some practice." She checked her watch again. "What are you doing here now, anyway?" she asked Lisa. "Not that I'm not always glad to see you and everything, but it's not exactly the weather for a leisurely Sunday afternoon trail ride."

"I had some free time, so I just thought I'd stop by and check on Prancer," Lisa replied.

She couldn't help smiling as she said the name of the beautiful bay Thoroughbred mare she'd ridden for the past few years. Prancer had started her life as a racehorse, but an injury had ended her career on the track. Max had recognized that the sweet-tempered young mare would make a wonderful pleasure horse, so he had bought her

4

in partnership with Judy Barker, the local equine vet, and brought her to Pine Hollow. Lisa had been the mare's most regular rider ever since, and over the years she had come to love the gentle, intelligent horse just as much as Carole and Stevie loved their own horses, Starlight and Belle. Recently Lisa had discovered that her father was planning to surprise her by buying Prancer for her next birthday. After all her years of riding, Lisa could hardly believe she was finally getting a horse of her own, let alone one as wonderful as Prancer. So far nobody else knew about the secret except Carole and Max, and Lisa could hardly wait until the day she was free to tell everyone her fantastic news.

"I guess I'll leave you to your work and go see her," Lisa added, already taking a step toward the stable aisle. Prancer usually spent much of the day outside in the little back paddock, but when the heavy rain started, Lisa was sure, someone would have brought her in. "Is she in her stall?"

"Um, not exactly," Carole said. "Remember those horses I mentioned before? The ones we turned out in the meadow this morning?"

"Prancer's out there?" Lisa frowned, surprised. Prancer was three and a half months pregnant with twins, which was a dangerous condition for a horse. Everyone at Pine Hollow was keeping a

5

close and cautious eye on her these days, especially since they'd all had a scare just a couple of weeks before, when Max had feared that the mare might have lost one of the foals.

Carole nodded. "Judy okayed it yesterday when she was here. She thinks Prancer could use a little more exercise, and she thought the hilly meadow would be perfect because she'd be less tempted to try to run there." She took a step toward the door, which was slightly ajar, revealing the pounding rain outside. Glancing back at Lisa, she shrugged. "I'm sure she's hiding out in one of the run-in sheds. You can walk out there and see her if you want, but you might want to take a life jacket along."

"Oh well. I guess my visit will have to wait." Lisa sighed, feeling disappointed. "As long as I'm here, I might as well make myself useful. Need any help with your chores?"

"Always," Carole answered. "I was just about to go pull Samson's mane and tail for the show, since I probably won't have a whole lot of spare time to do it later in the week. It would help a lot if you'd hold him for me. He's usually pretty good about stuff like that, but he hasn't been exercised yet today, so he may be frisky."

"No problem," Lisa said. "Sounds like a lot more fun than mucking out stalls."

Carole grinned. "You missed that—I just finished," she said. "But the great thing about mucking out is that no matter how often you do it, it always needs doing again before long."

Lisa laughed. She enjoyed most things about taking care of horses, but she had to admit that mucking out wasn't near the top of her list of favorite stable chores.

She followed Carole down the aisle to Samson's stall. The big black gelding had his head out over the half door and was watching their approach. Lisa couldn't help admiring the proud, intelligent gleam in his eyes and the high, aristocratic carriage of his muscular neck. *It's no wonder Carole is so crazy about him*, Lisa thought.

Carole greeted the gelding with a pat and a few murmured words. She and Samson had always shared a special bond—partly because she had once loved Samson's sire, a noble stallion who had been killed in a terrible riding accident years earlier, and partly because of Samson's own spirited, willing personality.

Lisa stood back as Carole expertly cross-tied Samson and gave him a pat. Then she stepped forward and stood at his head, holding his halter loosely with one hand and rubbing his smooth, dark neck with the other. "It's okay, big guy," she told the horse soothingly as Carole moved around to his side. "We're just going to get you gussied up for the big show next weekend."

Out of the corner of her eye, Lisa watched Carole pull a mane comb out of her jeans pocket. Moving to the top of Samson's crest, Carole carefully separated out a small cluster of hairs and held them in her left hand while she combed back the rest of the hairs with her right hand. "So what's new with you?" she asked Lisa as she worked.

"Alex and I got together Friday after his soccer match," Lisa said, tugging gently at Samson's halter as he tried to turn his head to see what Carole was doing. "So I finally got a chance to tell him about sending in that acceptance letter." Lisa couldn't help sighing slightly when she thought how she and her boyfriend, who also happened to be Stevie's twin brother, had to schedule time to see each other these days. That was because Alex and Stevie were both grounded for drinking at a party they'd had at their house while their parents were out of town. The only time Alex was allowed out of the house, except for school, was for soccer, so he and Lisa tried to meet after practices and games as often as they could. But it really wasn't often enough as far as Lisa was concerned.

"Oh, really?" Carole wrapped the smaller cluster of hairs around the mane comb a couple of times and, with a quick, expert motion, yanked them out. Samson didn't flinch, and Lisa gave him a pat. Carole glanced up before moving on to the next section of mane, looking curious. "What did he say?"

Lisa smiled. "Let's just say he was thrilled."

She could still see the overjoyed expression on Alex's face when she'd told him she had decided to attend Northern Virginia University, located just forty miles from Willow Creek. Lisa had come to the decision after receiving an early acceptance letter and offer of an honors scholarship from the well-respected local university. That decision had come as a relief—Lisa had spent a lot of time lately worrying about what she should do the following year. She had already applied to a couple of colleges in Southern California, where her father, stepmother, and baby half sister, Lily, lived. She'd also planned to apply to several prestigious schools in and around Boston and Chicago. But while each school on her list had advantages, most of them had major drawbacks as well. Attending college in California would mean being close to her father and having the chance to watch her half sister, Lily, grow up. And her California family would be there to help her find a place to board Prancer and to look after her during school breaks. But Lisa also knew that it would be very hard on her mother, who was still bitter about the divorce, to have her in California. Then there was Alex. Because he was only a junior this year, she would be separated from him for at least a year while he finished high school, and she knew that both of them would have a hard time with that.

Despite their academic benefits, the schools in the other cities seemed even more problematic. All the same issues would be there—distance from Alex, her mother, her friends, and everything she'd ever known, plus she wouldn't even have the advantage of being near Lily and her father. And it would be difficult to find a good boarding stable in a place where she didn't know a soul, especially since most of those schools were located in urban areas.

That was why the acceptance to NVU seemed like the perfect solution. Going to a local university meant she would still be able to spend time with Alex and her other friends in Willow Creek, particularly Carole and Stevie, who also had another year of high school to go. It also meant she wouldn't have to worry about where to keep Prancer. The mare could remain at Pine Hollow, where there were plenty of people to help Lisa look after her.

"Cool. So he took the news well." Carole shot her a quick glance. "What about your mom and dad? You never mentioned what they said about all this."

"That's because I haven't exactly told them

yet." Lisa sighed and rubbed Samson's nose. "I really want to talk to Mom about this first—you know how supersensitive she is about everything since the divorce. If I told Dad before I told her, she'd freak out and not even realize how great it is that I'll be staying close to home." She shrugged. "Besides, I figure I'll tell Dad when I see him in person at Thanksgiving."

Carole blinked. "Oh yeah. I almost forgot you're going out to California again. When are you leaving?"

"A week from Saturday." Lisa grimaced. "I just hope I get a chance to talk to Mom before then."

"What do you mean?" Carole asked uncertainly. "Did she go somewhere?"

Lisa chuckled ruefully. "No. Sorry, I'm just being silly. Mom's been so busy lately with her job and, you know, Rafe." The name, as always, left a bad taste in Lisa's mouth. She still found it hard to believe that her conservative, overcautious, forty-something mother was going out with a twenty-five-year-old loser like Rafe. It was even harder to believe that the two of them had been seeing each other for more than a month now.

Carole was silent for a moment as she pulled another section of Samson's mane. Then she glanced over at Lisa again. "You know, even

11

though Mom has been gone for years now, it's still always a little weird for me when Dad brings a new woman home," she said. "But one thing I've noticed over the years: Whenever he starts seeing someone I really don't like, it usually doesn't last long. Even or especially when I keep my opinion to myself."

Lisa didn't answer for a moment. She knew Carole was probably right. After all, Colonel Hanson had dated a variety of women over the years since his wife had died of cancer.

But Lisa's situation was different. Her father hadn't died. He had walked out on his wife of twenty-seven years, moved to California, and re-married. And her mother hadn't mourned her loss and then slowly, cautiously started to pick up the pieces and move on, as Colonel Hanson had done. Instead, she'd sunk into a lengthy period of depression and bitterness, then suddenly flung herself into a totally inappropriate relationship with a guy—Lisa couldn't bring herself to think of Rafe as a *man*—who was practically guaranteed to break her heart sooner or later, to say nothing of turning Lisa's stomach.

"Well, anyway," Lisa said at last, deciding to let Carole's well-intentioned advice pass without comment, "I'm planning to break the big news soon. Mom's off tomorrow night and I told her I wanted to fix a special dinner, just for the two of us. Rafe has a meeting with his adviser or something, so for once I hope I'll have her full attention."

"Doesn't Rafe go to NVU, too?" Carole asked.

Lisa shuddered. "Don't remind me," she said. "That's the only downside I can see to going there. But it's a big school, so it's not as if I'm likely to end up sitting next to him in class or anything." She grinned sheepishly. "Actually, I probably shouldn't admit this, but I'm sort of expecting—well, okay, *hoping*—that he'll flunk out by the time I start next fall."

Carole laughed, but she felt a little uncomfortable. Lisa's comment had reminded her of a topic she wished she could forget. A little more than a month earlier, Carole had failed a history test because she'd been so caught up with her job at Pine Hollow that she'd forgotten to study. She had convinced her teacher to give her a makeup test, claiming that her father had been ill. But Carole hadn't been any better prepared for the second test than she'd been for the first, so she had done something she never would have thought she was capable of doing. She had cheated. She had convinced herself that she'd had no choice—one of Max's strictest rules was that all his school-age riders had to keep their grades at a C average or above, and the failing grade would have pulled Carole's average below that cutoff. She knew she couldn't let that happen, especially with the Colesford show coming up. But ever since the moment she had opened her textbook and peeked at the answers, Carole had been forced to live with constant, nagging guilt over what she'd done. And she had been a lot more careful about keeping her grades up.

"Hey, as long as you're here," she said, glancing at Lisa over Samson's neck. "Do you know anything about the Great Depression?"

"Sure." Lisa shrugged. "We studied that last year in my American history class. I even wrote a term paper on it. Why?"

"Because I have a test on it in my American history class on Thursday." Carole forced a grin, not wanting her friend to guess why she was so worried about her history grade these days. She didn't ever want anyone to know about that. She only wished she could banish the whole incident from her own mind as well. "I guess this is the advantage of having a friend who's a year older, huh?"

"Hi! What are you guys doing?" came a cheerful, high-pitched voice from outside the stall. Glancing toward the aisle, Carole saw Maxine Regnery, Max's five-year-old daughter, peering around the half door. The little girl had inherited auburn hair and an inquisitive personality

14

from Max's wife, Deborah, who was a successful newspaper reporter. From her father, little Maxi had inherited bright blue eyes and a love of horses that had started seemingly before she could walk. Recently Max had been teaching Maxi how to ride on Pine Hollow's smallest pony, Krona.

"Hi, Maxi," Carole said with a slightly distracted smile. She was crazy about Maxi, but at the moment she wasn't in the mood for baby-sitting. She had too many other things to do. "What are you up to? Where's your dad?"

Maxi shrugged and let out a loud, exaggerated sigh. "He's *busy*," she said with a slight pout. "And I really, really, *really* want to go for a ride on Krona now."

"Now?" Lisa smiled. "But it's raining outside, silly. And Callie's in the indoor ring."

Maxi shrugged again. "The indoor ring's big," she said. "And Krona's little. We could ride there, too, and not bother anyone at all." She blinked at Lisa and smiled brightly. "All I need is someone to ride with me."

Carole had to stop herself from laughing. Maxi was awfully sly for a five-year-old.

"Sorry," Lisa said, patting Samson on the neck. "Carole and I have to finish up with good old Samson here. Maybe your dad will take you for a ride later."

"I don't think so." Maxi scowled unhappily. "Daddy said he's very busy today. He said he didn't have time to take me riding."

"Your daddy's not the only one who's busy. There's a big horse show next weekend, remember? So none of us will have a whole lot of spare time this week." Carole tried to stay patient with the little girl. She could still remember what it was like to be five years old and crazy about horses. "Maybe next week, after the show's over, we can go for a nice long ride together. How does that sound?"

"Okay," Maxi said, though she didn't seem too convinced. "What are you doing to Samson's mane?"

"I'm pulling it." Carole returned her attention to her task, separating out another cluster of coarse black hairs and wrapping them around the comb. "I need to thin it out so that it will lie flat and I can make it look nice for the horse show. I'm almost finished. See? Next I'm going to do his tail."

Maxi took a step closer and stared at Samson's mane for a moment. "It doesn't look any different to me," she announced solemnly at last.

Carole didn't bother to answer. She knew that Maxi was still too young to appreciate the subtle difference between a natural mane and a pulled one. But the judges at Saturday's show would notice every little detail, and even though the show jumping class she and Samson were entering would be judged on performance rather than appearance, Carole wanted the gelding to look his best. "Hey, Maxi, why don't you run up to the house now and find your mommy?" she suggested. "I'm sure she's wondering where you are."

Maxi shook her head until her reddish pigtails bounced. "She sent me here," she announced. "She's working."

"Well, watching us isn't going to be very interesting," Lisa said, leaning over long enough to tug gently on one of Maxi's pigtails. "So why don't you go watch Callie for a while? She's probably still riding in the indoor ring."

Maxi sighed sadly. "Okay," she muttered. "Bye."

"See you later," Lisa called after the little girl as she wandered off down the aisle. Then she turned to check on Carole's progress. "How's it going?"

"Fine," Carole reported. "I think I'm just about done with the mane." She stepped back and cocked a critical eye at her handiwork. "Ready to tackle the tail?"

Lisa nodded. "Against the door?"

"Better safe than sorry."

Carole walked along the horse's side, keeping

17

a hand on his back so that he could keep track of where she was. She opened the stall door and, once she was on the other side, closed it again between herself and the horse. Lisa positioned him so that his hindquarters were resting against the half door. Reaching over and giving him a quick pat on the rump, Carole grabbed his tail and slung it over the door so that it hung down over the other side. That way she could pull the tail with confidence, knowing she would be safe from Samson's hooves if he decided he wasn't enjoying her grooming efforts. The gelding cocked a suspicious ear back toward her, but as soon as Carole called out a few words of reassurance, he relaxed again.

"Wow," Lisa said, watching the horse. "He really trusts you."

"He knows I'd never hurt him," Carole said, patting the horse once more before brushing down the tail with her hand. She had hardly separated out the first few strands of long, coarse black hair when she and Lisa heard footsteps approaching. Carole glanced down the aisle, expecting to see Max searching for Maxi. Instead she spotted Ben Marlow walking toward them.

Ben was Pine Hollow's youngest full-time stable hand. Carole hadn't seen him yet that day, but she wasn't particularly surprised to see him now, even though Sunday was technically his

18

day off. Like her, he tended to show up at the stable every day whether he needed to be there or not. The two of them shared a deep passion for horses that meant they could only be truly content when they were taking care of their favorite creatures.

"How's it going, Ben?" Lisa said politely. "Are you ready for the show on Saturday?"

Ben answered with a shrug and an utterance that might have passed for an assent, though Carole couldn't help thinking that it sounded a lot more like a grunt.

Lisa nodded as if he'd actually responded. "You're entered in Open Jumping with Carole, right?"

"Yeah." Ben didn't even pretend to be interested in making small talk. His dark, deep-set eyes barely flickered over Lisa before transferring to Samson. He stepped over to shoo a fly from the gelding's withers, turning his back on Lisa.

Even the years of etiquette training Lisa had received from her mother couldn't stand up under Ben's brusque behavior. She rolled her eyes behind his back and poked one finger toward her throat, pretending to gag.

Carole blushed, wishing as she often did that her friends could look past Ben's reserved, suspicious, often downright hostile outer layer and catch a glimpse of what she sometimes saw un-

19

derneath. He might not have perfect manners or even be particularly likable much of the time, but he had a way with horses that Carole had never seen in anyone else, and that was enough to make her overlook any other faults. Besides, she was starting to suspect that Ben wasn't as completely indifferent to the people around him as he appeared. He had been the first to recognize that she was neglecting her own horse, Starlight, in favor of Samson, and he had helped her reach the difficult decision to try to sell Starlight and buy Samson from Max. She knew that hadn't been easy for him. He valued his own privacy so much that he was reluctant to get involved in anyone else's life. But he'd made the effort for her. Not only that, but he had also gone out of his way to help Carole keep her plan to sell Starlight a secret from everyone at Pine Hollow, including Max. He and Stevie and Lisa were still the only people who knew about her decision.

"Um, were you looking for me?" she asked Ben tentatively. Despite the recent advances in their friendship, she still was never quite sure how to act with him. She couldn't help remembering the awkward, humiliating moment when she had started to think that Ben might be interested in her as more than a friend. It had been at the party at Stevie's house a few weeks earlier.

Carole had asked Ben to dance, and he had responded by shooting her a look of stunned disbelief from beneath lowered brows, then stalking out of the room without a word or a backward glance.

"Max wants us to bring down some hay from the loft," he said gruffly, addressing his words to Carole and continuing to ignore Lisa completely.

"Okay. I'll come help as soon as I'm finished here, okay?" Carole shot Ben a rather anxious half smile, hoping he didn't turn around too quickly and catch Lisa, who was still making faces behind his back.

She found herself wishing once more that the *other* Ben—the kind, concerned Ben who made an effort to express himself, even if he wasn't very good at it—would appear more often. Maybe then she could figure out exactly how she was supposed to feel about him.

TWO

Stevie Lake glanced out the living room window. The rain was coming down in sheets, and she could barely see the mailbox at the end of the driveway.

"Ugh," she muttered under her breath. "There's nothing worse than a rainy Sunday. Unless it's a rainy Sunday when you've been grounded." She paused to consider her own statement for a moment. "Okay, except maybe a rainy Sunday when you're grounded and stuck doing stupid chores like dusting a bunch of furniture that isn't even dusty to begin with, and nobody else is even home to talk to." The family's dog, a lazy golden retriever named Bear, wandered into the room at that moment and gave Stevie a quizzical look. "You don't count," Stevie told him. "I can talk to you, but you don't talk back."

As Bear lowered himself to the rug with an exhausted sigh, Stevie pushed her dark blond

22

hair behind one ear and gave a halfhearted swipe at a small round table with the rag she was holding. Her gaze wandered to the rain-streaked window once again. Her only escape from her latest round of chores would be her trip to Pine Hollow to practice for the horse show. Her parents had allowed that one exception to her grounding. Stevie doubted the exception had anything to do with the fact that Colesford was by far the most competitive and prestigious show she'd ever entered, or that it was a huge honor—practically a miracle, really—that Max had asked her to join the elite group representing Pine Hollow. It probably had a lot more to do with the fact that Max had already paid the steep fee and sent in the paperwork necessary to enter Stevie and Belle in the show.

But Stevie wasn't the kind of person to worry too much about why they'd made the exception. She was just grateful that they had.

"I was going to wait until the rain let up," she told Bear thoughtfully, giving the table another careless swipe. "But I'm starting to think that could be, like, forty days and forty nights from now. And I don't have that much time to spare, you know?"

Just then the phone rang. Stevie turned away from the window and hurried over to the end table by the sofa to grab the receiver.

23

"Hello, Noah's Ark," she said. "Sorry, no vacancy."

"Not even for me?" a familiar voice replied.

"Phil!" Stevie's face relaxed into a smile at the sound of her longtime boyfriend's voice. She and Phil Marsten had met at riding camp when they were both in junior high, and they had been a solid couple ever since, despite the fact that they lived in different towns and attended different schools. Dropping her dust rag on the coffee table, she collapsed onto the sofa. "What's up?"

"Just calling to say hi and make sure you haven't floated away," Phil said cheerfully. "So what are you up to? Are you going to get in trouble for talking?"

"I'm the only one home," Stevie replied, leaning back against the sofa cushions and propping her feet on the coffee table. "Mom and Dad took Michael to the movies, and Alex is out picking up groceries or something."

"So poor Cinderella is home all alone," Phil said. "Discovered any great new ways to get your whites their whitest?"

"Hardy har har." Stevie snorted. "You're such a wit. A half-wit, that is."

"Your bitter, petty words can't possibly bring me down, my love," Phil said airily. "In case it's slipped your mind, today is my last day of solitary confinement."

24

That fact *had* slipped Stevie's mind. Phil had been drinking at her party, too, and his parents had grounded him for two weeks. "Lucky you," she said wistfully. "I've been grounded for so long that I've almost forgotten I ever had a life. What are you going to do to celebrate?"

"Well, my first choice would be to hang out with you," Phil said. "But I guess that's probably not going to work out, huh?"

"Not a chance." Stevie kicked at the dust rag with one foot, a sudden wave of self-pity sweeping over her. "My parents still won't even discuss when they might let up on us. My bet is sometime around Labor Day. In 2020."

Phil chuckled sympathetically. "Bummer," he said. "Just thought I'd ask. But anyway, since my number one choice of celebrating partners is still chained to her mop and broom, I figure I'll drag A.J. out. He could use a fun night out, too."

"That's great." Stevie couldn't help feeling a twinge of envy as she thought about Phil and his best friend, A. J. McDonnell, going out and having fun while she was stuck at home doing chores. Still, she tried to push those feelings aside and just be glad that the two friends would have some time to hang out. A.J. really could use some fun time with Phil after what he'd been through lately. "So has he decided what to do yet? About the adoption thing, I mean?"

"Not as far as I know." Phil's voice immediately sounded more subdued, as it usually did when discussing A.J.'s situation. "He still won't talk about it much. Not with me, and not with his folks, either."

"Too bad." Stevie shook her head, wondering how an open, friendly person like A.J. could shut out his friends so completely during such a confusing period in his life. She knew it had been a major shock for A.J. to discover that he was adopted. His parents had never said a word about it to him before. Still, wasn't that what friends were for? To help you through difficult times? "Maybe he'll loosen up while you're out tomorrow night. He's got to talk about this sooner or later, right?"

"I guess." Phil sighed. "Anyway, we're probably just going over to that diner in Berryville—you know, grab some food, play a few arcade games. Nothing major."

"Sounds like fun." Stevie tried to keep her tone light. It had been so long since she'd been able to hang out with Phil. She hadn't even seen him since the party, and she really missed him. "Hey, you're still coming to the horse show on Saturday, aren't you?"

"Definitely," Phil replied. "Especially if it could be my only chance to see you before

2020." His voice softened. "I miss you, you know."

"Me too." Stevie smiled, amazed as always at the way she and Phil often seemed to think the same thing at the same time. She glanced toward the window again. "I'd better go," she said reluctantly. "I've got to start thinking about heading over to Pine Hollow before it gets much later. I just hope it's not still raining when I get there. I'm sure Belle can swim, but I seriously doubt she can do dressage at the same time." She almost smiled as she tried to picture it. "Although if any horse could do it . . ."

Phil chuckled. "I know, I know," he said. "Belle the Wonder Horse can do anything."

"Have fun tomorrow night," Stevie said, trying to sound cheerful.

"I'll try," Phil replied. "But it won't be the same without you."

"Tell me about it," Stevie muttered as she hung up the phone. She was glad that Phil had called, but the conversation had left her feeling grumpy. Her grounding already seemed to have gone on forever. And now that Phil was going to be free again, it was going to be even harder to deal with being stuck at home all the time.

She was leaning over to retrieve her dust rag when she heard the front door open. Glancing at her watch, she saw that it was too early for her parents and younger brother to be returning from their movie. A moment later her twin brother, Alex, bounded into the room.

"Yo, sis," he said breathlessly, dropping a wet paper bag full of groceries on the sofa and another on the floor. "What's happening?"

Stevie grabbed the bag on the sofa. "Don't put that there!" she snapped. "It's soaked."

Alex shrugged. "What do you expect? It's pouring out there." He whistled as he slipped off his jacket and dropped that on the sofa, too.

Stevie rolled her eyes. Alex had spent the first week and a half of their grounding moping around constantly, complaining about how he never got to see Lisa. But ever since Lisa had broken the news about her college decision a couple of days earlier, Alex had been acting downright giddy.

"What are you so happy about?" Stevie asked sourly, scooping up his jacket and tossing it over a chair. "Don't tell me you're still all goofy because Lisa's staying local next year."

Alex dropped his keys and wallet on the coffee table, then flopped onto the sofa and grinned. "Hey, you've got to admit, it's pretty awesome news, right?"

"Awesome for *you*, maybe," Stevie muttered. Her brother's cheerfulness was really starting to wear on her nerves, especially since she wasn't sure that Lisa had done the right thing by sending in her acceptance to NVU so quickly.

Since when is sensible, super-logical Lisa Atwood so impulsive? she thought. *I mean, this is her whole future we're talking about here. She shouldn't have picked NVU just because it seemed like the easiest way to make everyone happy. And that's what it sounds like she did.*

Stevie hadn't said anything about her concerns to Lisa. There was really no point. By the time Lisa had told her what she'd decided to do, it was already done. The letter was in the mail, making it official. So why make her feel bad?

Still, she couldn't help feeling annoyed that Alex was so blindly happy about it. Didn't he even care that Lisa might be making a huge mistake? "You know," she told him, "if you really care about Lisa, you should be wondering right now if she's really doing what's best for her, not just getting all ecstatic because you got what *you* want."

Alex looked surprised. "What are you talking about?"

"I'm talking about Lisa's life," Stevie replied, putting her hands on her hips and gazing at him evenly. "I mean, you have to know that you're a big part of the reason she's so eager to stick around this area next year."

Alex frowned. "So? We want to be together,"

he said defensively, running one hand through his damp brown hair. "What's wrong with that?"

"What's wrong is that you've been acting totally possessive and obnoxious ever since she went to California last summer," Stevie said hotly. "You act like you'll die if she leaves your side for one tiny second. It's no wonder she's so worried about going away to school in California or wherever. You've made it pretty clear that the only thing you care about is having her here with you. That's pretty selfish, don't you think?"

"No," Alex shot back. But Stevie knew her twin well enough to read the hint of doubt in his hazel eyes.

She shrugged. "Well, I hope you can live with the guilt if she ends up wishing she'd thought about this more," she said. "Because I've known Lisa for a long time, and it's not like her to be so impulsive. Especially about something so important."

Alex barked out a short, humorless laugh. "That's pretty funny, coming from the queen of impulsiveness."

"We're not talking about me here," Stevie replied. She tossed her dust rag at him, feeling a little guilty for ruining his mood. Still, it was something he needed to hear. And who else was going to level with him? "I've got to go. If Mom and Dad get home before I do, tell them I'm at Pine Hollow."

Alex didn't respond. Stevie grabbed the car keys off the coffee table where he'd dropped them and hurried out of the room, leaving him sitting on the sofa with a thoughtful frown on his face.

"There you go, buddy." Callie Forester patted the black-and-white pinto fondly. "All clean again."

She had just finished grooming Patch, a gentle Pine Hollow school horse, after their therapeutic riding session. Callie appreciated having a reliable horse like Patch to work with, but she had to admit that she was getting a little bored with riding the unflappable pinto around and around the indoor ring. Still, she hadn't become a top-notch endurance rider by being impatient. She knew that the endless repetition of simple exercises was necessary if she wanted her leg to regain its full strength. But lately she had been itching for something a little more challenging, and she couldn't seem to stop herself from slipping into daydreams of tossing a saddle on one of Max's more spirited horses—Samson or Diablo or maybe the feisty young mare Firefly—and galloping off across the fields without looking back.

"Patience," she whispered to herself, giving

Patch one last scratch under the jawbone. "Don't make time the enemy." That was something her old endurance trainer back home had taught her. And she didn't plan to forget the lesson, especially now, when she was so close to getting what she'd worked for all these months. She adjusted her crutches under her arms and leaned over to unlatch the stall door.

Callie was letting herself out into the aisle when she spotted a small figure wandering slowly toward her. Maxi Regnery's usually cheerful face was downcast, and even the little girl's pigtails looked less jaunty than usual.

"Hey, Maxi," Callie called. "What's the matter?"

Maxi glanced up. "Hi, Callie," she said gloomily. "Are you busy, too?"

Callie wasn't sure what the little girl meant by that. She didn't have much experience with young children. Her only sibling was her older brother, Scott, and she'd never had much time for baby-sitting because of her training schedule. "Um, I'm not that busy," she said cautiously. "Why?"

Maxi shrugged. "Everybody else is busy," she explained. "Too busy for me. Mommy has a deadline. Everybody else is busy working, too. Daddy and Red and Denise and Carole and Lisa." She ticked off each name on her small

32

fingers, looking more dejected with each one. "And I really, really, really, *really* wanted to go riding." She sighed and blinked sadly at Callie. "Otherwise I'll probably forget everything Daddy taught me in my riding lessons."

"I doubt that will happen," Callie said, trying to sound cheerful and upbeat. "You're a terrific rider already, Maxi. You won't forget."

Maxi shrugged. "I might." She sighed noisily. "Anyway, there's nobody around to talk to me. Even Mini's taking a nap."

Callie couldn't help grimacing slightly at Maxi's younger sister's nickname. Three-year-old Jeanne Regnery had been called Mini practically since birth by just about everyone, despite her parents' best efforts to prevent the nickname from sticking. Fortunately, Mini herself didn't seem to mind.

"I'm talking to you, aren't I?" Callie told Maxi. "In fact, I have a great idea. I don't have to be anywhere in particular this afternoon. Why don't I check with your dad and see if it's okay for me to take you for a ride?"

Maxi's face lit up. "Really?" she cried.

"Really." Callie grinned at the little girl's obvious excitement. "Why don't you go get Krona's tack and wait for me at his stall? I'll be there in a minute."

"Thanks, Callie!" Maxi raced away in the direction of the tack room.

Fifteen minutes later, Maxi was leading her shaggy little half-Icelandic pony out of his stall. Max had okayed the riding lesson as soon as Callie had found him, seeming relieved that his daughter would be entertained. Callie had also checked in with Carole, who was helping Ben bring down hay. Knowing that her crutches could get in the way if any serious problems cropped up, she'd asked Carole to stay within shouting distance just in case.

Then, after a quick call to Scott, who was supposed to pick her up, Callie had hurried to help Maxi tack up. "You're really learning fast," she told the little girl as Maxi stepped confidently down the aisle with the pony following obediently at her shoulder. "Before long you'll be riding in horse shows just like—"

"Callie!" a breathless voice interrupted.

Callie looked up quickly, recognizing the voice. "George," she said, carefully keeping her voice neutral. "Hi."

George Wheeler hurried down the aisle toward her, a grin on his moon-shaped, slightly flushed face. "How's it going?" he asked her, ignoring Maxi, who had stopped Krona at Callie's side, looking annoyed at the interruption.

"Okay," Callie said blandly. She had been

feeling a little awkward around George all week. He was one of the best riders she'd ever known—so good that he and his horse, Joyride, were part of the select team going to the Colesford Horse Show the next weekend. But he was just as awkward and dumpy on the ground as he was graceful and confident in the saddle. Callie had tried to look past that when he'd asked her out recently. She had agreed to attend a school dance with him, but the evening hadn't gone very well, and Callie had ended up telling George a few days ago that she just wanted to be friends.

"So, did you finish those chemistry problems we were supposed to do this weekend?" George asked. "If you had any trouble with them, I could go over them with you."

"That's okay," Callie said. "I actually was going to do them tonight. But thanks anyway."

"Sure," George said eagerly. "If you want, I could call you later and see if you need any help, or—"

Maxi cleared her throat loudly, interrupting him. "It's probably not good for Krona to stand around in the aisle like this," she announced.

George blinked. Brushing his baby-fine blond hair off his forehead, he finally seemed to notice the little girl staring at him impatiently. "Oh, hey, Maxi," he said cheerfully. "Didn't see you there. So Callie's taking you for a ride, huh?"

"She *was*," Maxi said bluntly.

George raised an eyebrow and laughed. "Uh-oh," he joked, winking at Callie. "Guess that's a hint, huh? I'd better let you two get to it."

Callie returned his smile weakly, relieved to have such an easy excuse to escape. "Guess so," she said. "See you later, George."

"Bye." George stepped aside to let them pass, but Callie could practically feel his eyes on her back as she and Maxi walked down the aisle on either side of the pony.

Callie carefully kept her eyes on Maxi and Krona until she was sure they were all out of George's sight. Most of her conversations with him lately left her with a weird, unsettled feeling. George was being so friendly and cheerful whenever he saw her, it was almost as if their whole uncomfortable, awkward dating fiasco had never happened. *What's that about?* she wondered, not for the first time. *Does it mean he wasn't really that into me after all? Maybe he's happier just being friends, too.*

She managed to forget about George as she and Maxi entered the indoor ring. Like everything else in life, she figured that their relationship would settle itself, given enough time. Until then there wasn't much point in thinking about it.

For the next half hour, she and Maxi had a very pleasant time. Callie found that she enjoyed playing teacher, sharing with the eager little girl some of what she'd learned about riding over the years. And Maxi was a fast learner—despite her young age, she seemed to instantly absorb every tip or tidbit that Callie shared.

Callie was watching Krona trot slowly around the ring, Maxi posting up and down smoothly and evenly in the pony's saddle, when Deborah appeared in the doorway. Her three-year-old daughter was hovering shyly at her heels. Unlike her extroverted older sister, Mini Regnery was rather quiet and shy; she seemed especially intimidated by the sheer size of the horses in the stable.

"Mommy!" Maxi cried when she spotted them, waving wildly from Krona's saddle. "Mini! Look at me! Callie taught me how to keep my hands still when I post."

"Let's stop for a minute," Callie told Maxi. She gathered her crutches and swung toward Deborah with a tentative smile. "I was just giving Maxi a little riding practice," she said. "I hope that's okay with you. Max said it would be all right."

"Of course." Deborah smiled back at her.

"I'm so grateful that you've been keeping her out of Max's hair. He's so busy with this horse show, and I'm crazed with a deadline. . . . Let's just say we can use all the volunteer baby-sitters we can get right now." She winked at Callie, then called to Maxi. "Come on, sweets. It's time for you to come up to the house and help me get dinner started."

"Are you sure, Mommy?" Maxi replied, looking disappointed. "Because I'm not even hungry yet."

"I'm hungry," Mini piped up.

Deborah smiled at the younger girl and ruffled her soft blond hair. "Me too," she said. "Come on, Maxi. Time to let Callie go, okay? Hop down from there and I'll help you put your pony away."

"Oh, okay. But Mommy, Callie's been teaching me everything!" Maxi climbed down from Krona's saddle and rushed over to her mother, leaving the well-mannered pony ground-tied. "She knows everything!"

"Is that right?" Deborah bent down to give her daughter a hug, shooting Callie a bemused smile over the little girl's head. "I'll have to keep that in mind next time I need to research an article."

Callie laughed. "Sorry. The only thing I know

about is riding," she said. "And Max is much more of an expert on that than I am."

"Callie, Callie, can we go riding again sometime?" Maxi begged. She grabbed Callie's arm and yanked on it eagerly, almost unbalancing her. "Pretty please?"

"Well, when you put it that way, how can I say no?" Callie smiled as she gently pulled her arm free and shifted her crutches to regain her balance.

Deborah grabbed Maxi and pulled her to her side. She gave Callie a searching glance. "Are you sure you have time for that, Callie? I know you're pretty busy with school and your therapeutic riding and everything. I'm sure Maxi will understand if you don't have time this week."

"It's no problem. Really," Callie assured her. "I'd love to do this again soon." She leaned over to meet the little girl's eye. "How about Wednesday afternoon? Want to get together then?"

Maxi looked slightly disappointed. "But that's . . ." She paused to count on her fingers. "Um, four days away?"

"Three days away," Deborah corrected gently. "Today's Sunday. Then there's Monday, Tuesday, and then Wednesday. Three days."

"Three days away," Maxi said, unfazed by the correction. "That's so long!"

"Sorry." Callie smiled as it occurred to her

39

that she and Maxi weren't so different in some ways, despite the gap in their ages. Maxi was as impatient to go riding again as Callie was to walk without her crutches. Patience was a tough sell at any age. "I have to go see my doctor tomorrow," she explained. "And then Tuesday my family is going to Washington to visit some friends. But I'll have plenty of free time on Wednesday. We can go for a nice long ride then, okay? Maybe if it's not raining, we can ride Patch and Krona around in the back paddock. We could meet around four o'clock. How does that sound?"

"That sounds perfect," Deborah said gratefully. "Maxi, why don't you go put your pony back in his stall now? I'll come and help you with the tack in a second."

"Okay." Maxi went over to retrieve Krona, leading him out of the ring and chattering to him all the while about how much fun they were going to have on Wednesday with Callie.

Callie smiled as the little girl disappeared around the corner of the doorway. "She's really adorable," she told Deborah. "I haven't spent much time with little kids before, but we really had fun today."

"I can tell. It looks like she's pretty smitten with you," Deborah said with a chuckle. "And I have to tell you, I really do appreciate your offering to spend more time with her. That killer deadline I mentioned is going to keep me busy all week. Jeannie's happy playing quietly with her toys while I work, but that one . . ." She gestured in the direction Maxi had gone with a fond smile. "She's just like her father. Never content unless she's here at the stable messing around with the horses. Usually Max doesn't mind having her tag along, but he's so frantic this week getting ready for that horse show . . ." She grinned sheepishly. "Well, as I started to say before, basically any time we can con someone else into looking after Maxi for a little while is a godsend."

"I'm glad I can help," Callie said with a smile.

THREE

Lisa hummed softly as she opened the oven and peeked inside. The warm scent of the baking potatoes mingled with that of the roasted chicken cooling on the counter nearby, making Lisa's stomach grumble. It was Monday evening, and Mrs. Atwood was due home any minute from her shift at the clothing store where she worked as an assistant manager. Lisa wanted everything to be ready. She was looking forward to finally telling her mother about her college decision.

She's going to be just as thrilled as Alex was, if not more, Lisa thought happily, closing the oven door and hurrying to the refrigerator to see if the iced tea she'd made was chilled yet. Pouring herself a glass, she perched on the edge of a chair at the kitchen table, which was neatly set with two places.

She sipped her iced tea, feeling herself relax. It had been surprisingly satisfying to spend the afternoon cooking for the two of them again. From the time her father had walked out until Mrs. Atwood had started seeing Rafe, Lisa had been forced to take on a lot of the household duties, cooking and cleaning and taking care of both of them because her mother had been too sunk in her own bitterness to handle the responsibility. Lisa didn't miss those days—her mother's return to something like normal life was the one reason she was grateful to Rafe—but it was still nice to do something for the two of them once in a while.

"Mmm!" Her mother's voice rang out from the front hall, interrupting her thoughts. "Lisa? Something smells wonderful!"

"Thanks," Lisa called back. "I told you I'd make something special for tonight, didn't I?" She hopped up and hurried toward the doorway with a smile on her face.

But she stopped short when she saw the tall, languid but good-looking young man with longish curly dark hair who was following her mother.

"Yo," Rafe said with a lazy grin. "Let me guess. We're having chicken, right?"

Lisa frowned. "But what—" she began before she could stop herself. Then she swallowed the impolite question—"What are you doing here?"—knowing it would only annoy her

43

mother. "Um, Mom told me you were busy tonight. With your adviser or something."

Rafe shrugged, his grin never faltering. "You know how it is," he said. "College life. People are always changing their plans. You just gotta go with the flow."

Lisa wasn't sure that explained anything, but she didn't really care why Rafe wasn't with his adviser. The only thing that concerned her was that he was here, now, ruining her special evening with her mother. "I didn't know you were coming," she said with barely concealed ill grace. "I don't know if there's enough food for three."

"Don't be silly, sweetie," Mrs. Atwood said. "I'm sure there's plenty. And anyway, I'm not that hungry. Rafe took me out to lunch today, and I ate so much I thought I would burst."

"You did not." Rafe reached over and pinched Mrs. Atwood's stomach. "You ate like a bird, like always."

"Rafe!" Mrs. Atwood squealed, batting his hand away. "That tickles."

Rafe grabbed her by the waist and started tickling her in earnest. "Oh yeah? How about this?"

Lisa averted her eyes as her mother shrieked and laughed at the same time, hardly even trying to push him away. It was unbearable to watch her mother and Rafe giggle and hang on each other all the time like a couple of teenagers.

Worse that that, actually, she thought grimly. *My friends and I are teenagers, and we all have enough class not to grope each other in public.*

"I'd better go take the potatoes out of the oven," she said, turning back toward the kitchen. "And set another place," she added pointedly.

Her mother and Rafe didn't respond, and Lisa didn't bother glancing back to see if they'd even heard her. She headed for the oven, feeling peevish. She had planned this evening so carefully—why did Rafe have to barge in and ruin everything? There was no way Lisa could share her news with her mother now. Not in front of him.

When her mother and Rafe entered the kitchen, they were both smiling and slightly flushed. Lisa did her best to act normal as she carried another plate and glass over to the butcher-block kitchen table. She had purposely set their places there instead of at the larger, more formal cherry table in the dining room, wanting it to be a casual, intimate meal. Now she wished she could switch the dinner into the dining room, where she could put more distance between herself and Rafe. But it didn't seem worth the effort.

"Everything's just about ready," she told her mother. "Why don't you sit down? I'll bring the food over to the table."

"Thanks, sweetie." Her mother patted her on

the cheek and then took a seat beside Rafe, who was already sprawled in his chair. "By the way, what's the occasion? I forgot to ask yesterday. You said this would be a very special dinner."

"Nothing." Lisa turned away and busied herself with the platter of chicken. "Nothing at all."

Later that night Stevie was getting ready for bed when the phone rang. It was the line that served the phone on her own bedside table as well as the extension in her twin's room and the one in the hall outside the bathroom. She glanced at the clock.

"Eleven-fifteen," she muttered. "Who would be calling at this hour?"

Someone else picked up after one ring. *It's probably Lisa calling for Alex*, Stevie thought, picking up her hairbrush and staring at her reflection in the mirror over her dresser. *Maybe she's calling to tell him she decided to forget about NVU and enroll at Cross County Community College so that she can be even closer to him next year.* She still felt a little bit guilty about taking out her worries on her brother the previous day, but she thought it was about time that somebody pointed out the truth to him.

A few seconds later Mrs. Lake poked her head into Stevie's bedroom. "It's for you," she said, gesturing to the phone. "Phil."

Stevie blinked in surprise. "Is it okay if I talk to him?" she asked uncertainly. Her parents were being pretty strict about her phone privileges because of her grounding. But even under normal circumstances, they frowned on phone calls after ten-thirty.

Mrs. Lake nodded. "Make it quick, though, okay?"

"Sure. Thanks, Mom." Stevie hurried to pick up the phone. "Phil?" she said. "Hi, it's me."

"Hey. I'm glad you can talk."

Stevie could tell right away that something was wrong. Phil's voice sounded odd and fuzzy, the way it did when he was really upset. "What is it?" she demanded. "What's the matter?"

"I just got back from my big night out," Phil said. "With A.J."

Stevie perched on the edge of her bed. "Did something happen?"

Phil sighed into the phone. "A lot of stuff happened," he said heavily. "To start with, A.J. brought a flask along."

"A what?" For a split second, Stevie didn't understand what he was talking about. Then she gasped. "Wait—you mean as in *alcohol*?"

"You got it," Phil said grimly. "Vodka, to be specific. He was spiking his sodas all night. I didn't notice at first—that stuff doesn't really have a smell, you know—and by the time I

47

caught him doing it, he was already pretty wasted."

"How could you not notice!" Stevie exclaimed, remembering how odd and hyper A.J. had acted at her party, where he'd started everyone drinking after discovering some beer in the Lakes' garage.

"He hasn't exactly been acting like himself lately, you know," Phil replied. "I thought he was just feeling weird about hanging out. You know, it's the first time we've spent time together since the party—outside of school, I mean."

"Okay. Sorry." Stevie chewed on her lower lip, gripping the phone tightly as she tried to figure out what to think about this. "So did you try to talk him into laying off?"

Phil sighed again. "Of course I did," he said. "But he's gotten really good lately at not listening to anything anybody tries to tell him."

"Wow." Stevie shook her head. "So what did you do?"

"I kept trying to talk some sense into him," Phil said, "until I came back from the bathroom and took a sip of my soda. It tasted a little strange, but I probably would have just thought it was flat or something. Except that, as you know, A.J. has never been able to keep a straight face. And he's even worse when he's drunk."

"What?" Stevie gasped. "You mean he spiked *your* soda, too?"

"Uh-huh. Nice, huh? Especially since I was driving tonight. It's just lucky I caught him before I'd taken more than a sip or two."

Stevie sank back onto her bed, feeling more disturbed than ever by A.J.'s behavior. It was bad enough that he was being reckless with his own life. After all, he was only sixteen: If anyone caught him drinking in public, he could be in a lot of trouble. But it was even worse to hear that he was willing to put Phil at risk, too. *The old A.J. wouldn't have done that*, Stevie thought. *The old A.J. was a good friend and a good person. I'm starting to think that I don't know this new A.J. at all. And I'm definitely thinking I don't like him much.*

Still, she knew she couldn't give up on A.J. yet. Not when there was still a chance of helping him get back to normal. "What did you do then?" she asked Phil.

"I talked him into passing me the flask," Phil said. "I pretended I wanted a swig. Then I dumped it out in the vase of flowers on the table." He laughed briefly. "Luckily the flowers were plastic."

"Was he mad?"

"Not really. The flask was almost empty by then anyway." Phil sighed. "And he was so drunk that he just thought it was funny. He kept calling me 'Officer' for the rest of the evening— you know, like I was the cops or something. He thought that was really funny." He cleared his throat. "Finally I told him I was tired, and I dropped him off at home. That was a few minutes ago. I still feel like I should have done something more, though. I mean, after what happened at your party . . ."

"You did what you could," Stevie said, trying to sound reassuring. "Anyway, try not to worry too much. This probably doesn't mean anything. He's obviously still having trouble dealing with his parents, and so he decided to—"

She cut herself off as her mother stuck her head in the room again and gave her a pointed look. Stevie gulped and glanced at the clock.

"Whoops," she said. "I have to go. I'm sorry."

"It's okay," Phil said. "Sorry for calling so late, but I'm just feeling kind of freaked, you know?"

"I know." Stevie shot her mother an apologetic smile. Mrs. Lake cocked one eyebrow sternly before backing out of the room. "Maybe we can talk about this some more when we see each other at the horse show on Saturday, okay?"

"Okay. Thanks for listening," Phil said softly. "I love you, Stevie."

Stevie felt a lump form in her throat. How

long had it been since he had said those words to her face, instead of through the impersonal distance of a phone line? "I love you, too."

She waited for the click from the other end of the line before she hung up. Then she crawled into bed and pulled the covers up to her chin. She still wasn't sure what to think about A.J.'s drinking, but she did know one thing: If she didn't get to see Phil soon—feel his arms around her, his kiss on her lips—she would go crazy.

Lisa looked up from her French homework and glanced at her watch when she heard the front door slam. Eleven-thirty. *It's about time*, she thought irritably, standing up from her desk and stretching. *I thought he was never going to leave.*

She had excused herself from the dinner table as early as possible, claiming that she had a lot of homework. Her mother and Rafe had been so busy giggling over something stupid their boss had said at work that they'd hardly seemed to notice her departure.

Eventually Lisa had heard the sound of their voices as they moved from the kitchen into the living room. After that there had been an occasional burst of laughter or loud conversation. In between were long periods of quiet, which were even worse. Lisa hated the feeling of being afraid

51

to walk around her own house without stumbling across something she really, really didn't want to see.

Pushing those thoughts out of her head, Lisa hurried downstairs and found her mother puttering around the kitchen. "Hi," Lisa said. "Did Rafe go home?"

"He just left." Mrs. Atwood opened a cabinet and pulled out a clean glass. Heading to the refrigerator, she poured herself a glass of iced tea from the pitcher, which was almost empty. "Thanks again for making such a nice dinner tonight, sweetie. I think Rafe had a really nice time. He thinks you're wonderful, you know." She smiled and patted Lisa's cheek on her way to the table. "Almost as wonderful as I do."

"That's nice." Lisa smiled blandly, willing herself to let the comment pass. This evening might not have gone quite the way she'd planned, but she still wanted to share her news with her mother before any more time passed. "Listen, Mom. I actually do have something important to tell you. I just didn't want to say anything before, while, um, we had company."

Mrs. Atwood settled herself in her chair and took a sip of her tea. "What is it, dear?"

Lisa sat down across from her. "It's sort of important. I think you'll be really happy." She felt a flutter of nervousness, though she wasn't sure why. What she was about to announce was guaranteed to make her mother's good mood even better. "It's about college."

"What about it?" Mrs. Atwood asked pleasantly.

Lisa took a deep breath. "I decided where I'm going next year," she said. "I'm going to Northern Virginia U."

"That's nice, dear," Mrs. Atwood said. "But why don't you wait until you hear back from all the schools you applied to before you make up your mind? After all, you don't have to reply until spring."

"I already replied," Lisa said. "I replied to NVU. I told them I was coming."

Mrs. Atwood frowned, looking confused. "What are you talking about? You haven't even been accepted yet. I'm sure you will be, of course, but—"

"Yes I have," Lisa interrupted. "I have been accepted. I got the letter about a week ago. I forgot to show it to you when it came—sorry."

"Wait a minute." Mrs. Atwood pushed her glass away so quickly that some of its contents sloshed over the side onto the table. "Are you saying what I think you're saying? You got accepted to NVU and you forgot to tell me? And you already sent back notice that you're going there?"

"That's right." Lisa smiled tentatively. Her mother didn't seem to be following what she was saying too well. "I mailed back the form last week. Isn't that great? It's all settled."

Mrs. Atwood didn't speak for a second. Her brown eyes blinked rapidly a few times. "Are you crazy!" she exclaimed.

"What?" Lisa was startled and dismayed. "What do you mean? I thought you'd be happy."

"Happy?" Mrs. Atwood cried, sounding horrified. "How could I be happy that you did this—made such an important, life-changing decision without even consulting me?"

"I wasn't trying to leave you out. It's just that when I realized how perfect NVU is for me, I couldn't wait to send back my response."

Mrs. Atwood shook her head grimly. "And I suppose you couldn't wait to think about it a little longer, either?"

Lisa gripped the edge of the table. "I *did* think about it," she insisted. She really didn't understand why her mother was reacting this way. This was supposed to be *good* news. "I thought about it a lot. And I really think I made the right decision."

"Well, this is awful. Just awful," Mrs. Atwood declared, talking more to herself than to Lisa. "I can't believe you could do something like that without even telling me." She narrowed her eyes and stared at Lisa suspiciously. "Your father didn't put you up to this, did he?"

Lisa grabbed her head, wondering exactly when she'd wandered through the looking glass. Her mother was so upset that she wasn't even making sense. Why would her father, who lived in California, scheme behind his ex-wife's back to get Lisa to go to a college in Virginia? "Of course not," she said. "He doesn't know anything about it yet."

"Never mind him," Mrs. Atwood said grimly. "He'll never need to know about this little fiasco if we can figure out a way to undo it."

Lisa stood up. She could feel her hands starting to shake. "What's wrong with you?" she cried. "You're acting like this is some tragedy. Don't you understand what I'm telling you? I don't *want* to undo it. I made up my mind. I want to go to NVU!"

Mrs. Atwood took a deep breath. "Why don't you go up to bed now, Lisa?" she said evenly. "We can discuss this further tomorrow. After I've had a chance to take it in."

"Fine." Lisa headed for the stairs and rushed up to her room, feeling shaken and confused.

What was wrong with her mother? She had no idea, but she hoped she got over it soon. Because Lisa had already decided she was going to NVU, and her mother was just going to have to accept it.

FOUR

Carole dropped Samson's face sponge into her grooming bucket and gave him one last pat on the neck. "Good practice today, big guy," she told the gelding fondly.

Samson ignored her, seeming much more interested in his hayrack than in her words of praise. Carole smiled and let herself out of the stall, leaving him to his snack. Slinging his tack over her arms, she headed down the aisle.

When Carole entered the tack room, Stevie looked up from scrubbing Belle's saddle. "Hey," she said. "Did you just finish with Samson?"

"Uh-huh," Carole replied, setting her saddle on the rack beside Stevie's. "He did really well today. But I still can't believe the show is only four days away."

Stevie snorted. "Tell me about it. I'm getting so nervous that Belle is starting to give me funny looks."

"You? Nervous?" As she hung Samson's bridle

from a handy hook, Carole cocked a surprised eye at her friend. Stevie wasn't usually the type to suffer from stage fright, before a horse show or at any other time. "I don't believe it."

"What can I say?" Stevie shrugged and rubbed her sponge on a bar of saddle soap. "This show's a pretty big deal, you know. And it's not as if Belle and I are natural superstars the way you and Samson are."

Carole felt herself blush. "We're not—"

"Besides," Stevie interrupted before she could finish protesting. "Practically everyone I know is going to be there. Kids at school keep stopping me to ask what time the show starts. I think everyone in town is planning to attend."

"Tell me about it." Carole grinned. "Even a couple of my teachers are talking about coming. Mr. Whiteside—he's my algebra teacher—said he wants to be able to say he knew me when."

Stevie grinned back. "I'll be doing more than saying it," she said. "When you're some famous Olympic champion someday, I'll be selling your old e-mails and postcards to the highest bidder."

Carole laughed and gave her a playful shove. "Stop it. Now pass me the saddle soap and tell me what else is new."

"Okay." Stevie's expression sobered. "I've been thinking a lot about Starlight. You know, about finding the perfect buyer."

Carole felt her heart skip. It was still hard for her to think about what she was planning to do—to sell the horse that had been such a huge part of her life for so many years. That was one reason she'd asked Stevie to help her track down a buyer. "Did you come up with anything?"

"Maybe," Stevie said. "You know Rachel Hart, right?"

"Of course." Rachel was a member of the intermediate riding class at Pine Hollow and a seventh-grader at Fenton Hall. "What about her?"

Stevie shrugged. "I remembered that Michael mentioned a while ago that she was hoping to get her own horse for her birthday next month," she said. "They're in the same class, remember?"

Carole nodded. "So do you think Rachel would be interested in buying Starlight?" She felt a flash of hope. She hadn't even dared to imagine that she might find a buyer for Starlight right there at Pine Hollow. It would be the perfect solution. She would still be able to see him, maybe even ride him once in a while. And she would be able to make sure that he was being well taken care of. Not that she would have much to worry about if Rachel bought him. She was one of the most thoughtful and responsible students in the intermediate class. Besides that, she was an awfully good rider, and getting better all the time. She and Starlight would be a wonderful match.

Stevie shrugged. "I haven't said anything to her yet," she said. "But I did a little asking around, and she's definitely planning to hit her parents up with the horse idea soon. It's all her friends can talk about."

Carole nodded thoughtfully, leaning over to fish a cloth out of a basket near the wall. As she dipped it into the water bucket at Stevie's feet, she couldn't help feeling a twinge of nostalgia at the thought that Starlight could soon be a special birthday gift for someone else. He had been the most wonderful Christmas present she had ever received. But she tried not to dwell on the past. She was trying to secure the best future for both of them. And if she was lucky, her own future might include another very special gift someday soon. She was hoping that once Starlight's sale was complete, she could convince her father to chip in at least some of the extra money it would take to buy Samson from Max. Carole's seventeenth birthday was coming up the following week, and then Christmas was just six weeks or so later. . . .

"But that's not all," Stevie said, shoving aside the water bucket as she moved around to tackle the other side of Belle's saddle. "I talked to that girl last night—you know, the one my cousin told me about? I mentioned her the other day."

"I remember." Carole squeezed the excess water out of her cloth, hardly noticing when half of it dribbled down her arms. "You said she's like fourteen or so, and she lives somewhere sort of near here, right?"

"Her name's Tanya," Stevie reported. "She lives over in Mendenhall—you know, that town a few miles past Berryville. I told her all about Starlight, and she's really interested. Do you want to talk to her?"

Carole gulped and absently ran the damp cloth she was holding over the cheek strap of Samson's bridle. It was harder to think about selling her beloved Starlight to a total stranger than passing him along to someone she already knew and trusted right there at Pine Hollow. Still, she knew she had to be practical about this. If Rachel didn't pan out, she would need a backup buyer. "Okay," she said. "Go ahead and give her my number. Oh, and feel free to talk to Rachel about Starlight if you want. Just make sure you swear her to secrecy. I don't want anyone, especially Max, to hear about this until I'm ready to tell him."

Stevie nodded. For a moment the two friends worked in silence, each thinking her own thoughts. Carole wasn't sure what Stevie was pondering, but for her own part, she couldn't seem to stop thinking about Starlight and Samson. Samson and Starlight. It didn't seem fair that she had to choose between them when they were both so wonderful in their own way. But she knew there was no way she could give enough attention to both of them. Maybe someday, when she was spending all her time working with horses, she would be able to handle more than one mount. But not now, when school still took up so much of her time.

Finally Carole decided to take her mind off that subject. She had enough to worry about this week, between her job, preparing for the show, and passing her big history test in two days. "Hey, have you seen Lisa today? I wonder if she told her mom about her college thing. Last I heard she was planning some big dinner last night."

Stevie shrugged. "I haven't seen her in days. You're the one who goes to the same school as her."

"True. But we don't even have the same lunch period this year, let alone any classes." Carole hesitated for a moment, pretending to concentrate on scraping a speck of dirt off Samson's noseband. She wasn't sure how to bring up the topic that had been nagging at her ever since

Lisa's big announcement. "Um, so what do you think of Lisa's news? About NVU, I mean."

Stevie lowered her sponge and turned to face Carole, shooting her a searching look. "Well, now that you ask," she said, "I've actually been thinking about it a lot. And most of what I've been thinking is that she may have made a colossal blooper."

Carole was relieved to hear her say that. Stevie's older brother, Chad, went to NVU, and Carole didn't want her friend to think that she was putting down his school if she brought up her concerns about Lisa's decision. "Me too," she said. "I mean, at first I thought it was great. It seemed like the perfect solution. She would still be around, so we could hang out with her almost as much as always. And it would be good for her mother, too, I guess, and of course Alex. . . ." She almost added Prancer to the list, but she stopped herself just in time. Stevie still didn't know that Lisa's father was buying her the mare, and Carole had learned the hard way that it was better not to blurt out other people's secrets.

Stevie nodded vigorously. "I know. But is it going to be good for Lisa herself? As good for her as those other schools she was thinking about, I mean? I'm not so sure." She shrugged. "Don't get me wrong. I certainly wasn't looking forward to having her go off halfway across the country. But I also don't want her to stick around just to keep me happy, you know?" She fell silent for a moment. "I'm not sure Alex feels the same way, though."

"Alex loves her," Carole reminded her. "I'm sure he wants what's best for her."

Stevie cleared her throat. "Yeah, I know," she said quietly. "I kind of got on his case about it the other day, and I could tell he hadn't really thought about it that much except to be glad that he and Lisa could still be together next year. I think he felt kind of bad when I told him he was being selfish and that Lisa could end up regretting this if she really did this just because she was afraid he'd freak out if she went away to school."

"I feel bad about talking about this behind her back," Carole said. "I wish we could just come out and say something to her. But I'm not sure what good it would do."

"I know." Stevie chewed on her lip for a second, then shrugged. "I thought about that, too. She already sent in that acceptance thingie. I think that means she's pretty much stuck going there. So it's a little late for any of us to start talking to her about this now, right?"

Carole didn't like the thought that it was too late for Lisa to change her mind if she wanted to.

"I guess," she said. "Still, there must be a way she could get out of it if she had to. I mean, what if she got really sick or joined the army or something? It's not like they could *force* her to go there, right?"

Stevie shrugged again. "Don't ask me," she said. "I have no idea how these things work. But I'm willing to bet it would be a hassle for her to change her mind now."

Before Carole could answer, she heard footsteps approaching. Glancing at the door, she saw Ben entering the tack room. He paused just inside. "Carole," he said in his low, gruff voice, "Max wants you. Bandages."

Carole gasped, suddenly remembering that today was the day she'd promised to help Max and the others gather the traveling bandages and other equipment they would need for transporting the horses to Saturday's show. "Oops!" she said. "I totally forgot about that. I'm coming." She hopped to her feet before noticing that she was still holding a damp rag and remembering that she'd barely made a start at cleaning Samson's bridle. She hadn't touched his saddle at all.

Stevie caught her expression and read her mind. "I'll finish up your tack if you want," she offered. "Go ahead. It's okay."

"Thanks," Carole said gratefully, dropping

her rag on Samson's saddle and heading out after Ben. "I owe you one."

As she emerged into the hallway, Carole glanced at her watch, feeling guilty. She couldn't believe that those stupid bandages had totally slipped her mind. Worse, she'd spent far too much time sitting around the tack room gossiping with Stevie—time that she'd planned to spend taking Prancer for a walk. With all the preshow excitement, the pregnant mare had been all but ignored lately.

"Tell Max I'll be there in, like, two seconds, okay?" she told Ben. "I just have to take care of one quick thing first."

Ben nodded and headed down the hall toward the supply closet. Carole turned the opposite way, hurrying across the entryway into the stable aisle. She paused halfway down, in front of the pregnant mare's stall. Prancer was standing near the back wall, nosing halfheartedly at her water bucket. "Hey, sweetheart," Carole called softly. "I just stopped by to see how you're doing today."

Prancer didn't move except to swing her head toward the girl and let out a snort. Then she stamped one foot and rolled her eyes before turning away from Carole again.

Carole checked her watch again, wishing there were more hours in a day. Prancer seemed restless, which meant she probably would have really appreciated getting out of her stall for a little while. Still, there wasn't much Carole could do about it right then except to turn her out in the back paddock where she could at least move around a little on her own.

"Don't worry, Prancer," she said soothingly as she unlatched the stall door. "Next week, after the show is over, I'll take you for a nice long walk every day. And I'll let you graze as much as you want on the way. How does that sound?"

Prancer pinned her ears back and stamped her foot again, shifting away from Carole and shaking her head. Carole moved smoothly with her and soon had her under control. She led her out of the stall and down the aisle to the back entrance. Unlatching the paddock gate, she led Prancer through and slipped off her halter.

"There you go, girl," she murmured, patting Prancer on the side. The mare shied away and shook her head. Swallowing another pang of guilt, Carole turned and hurried out of the paddock, vowing once again to pay a lot more attention to the pregnant mare as soon as the horse show was over.

Meanwhile, Stevie was taking her time with Samson's tack. She was in no hurry to return home to more chores. It amazed her that her parents could continue to come up with enough dull and/or disgusting tasks to keep her and Alex busy every single day.

While she worked, she thought about Starlight's potential buyers. She could tell that Carole was pretty broken up about her decision to sell him. In fact, Stevie got a little misty when she thought about it herself. Starlight had become a familiar fixture in all of their lives. Still, she wanted to help her friend as much as she could. And if that meant finding a new home for Carole's horse, Stevie was going to do her very best to find the perfect new owner.

She made a mental note to call her cousin's contact from the stable pay phone on her way out. Tanya had sounded really enthusiastic about Starlight when Stevie had spoken to her the first time. Naturally, that didn't necessarily mean the girl was going to want to buy him once she rode him. People needed to click with their horses, and there was no way to tell if that was going to happen until they met face-to-face. Still, Starlight was such a good-natured, willing mount that Stevie was sure he could win over just about anyone, including Tanya.

Then there was Rachel Hart. Stevie didn't know the younger girl that well, but she'd seen her around Pine Hollow often enough to know that she was a good rider and a nice person. And with her birthday coming up . . .

Thinking about Rachel's birthday suddenly reminded Stevie that Carole's birthday was approaching rapidly. *Yikes*, she thought, calculating quickly in her head. *Today's Tuesday, which means it's less than a week away—next Monday, to be exact. And I have no idea what to get her.*

She dropped her sponge and sat back for a moment, stretching her fingers and thinking. It was never that hard to shop for Carole—she would appreciate just about anything that had to do with horses. Stevie knew she could just stop by the local tack shop and pick up something there—a new pair of string gloves, a horse sweatshirt or coffee mug, even a gift certificate. But those ideas didn't really satisfy her. With everything that Carole was going through right now with Starlight and Samson, Stevie wanted to get her something a little more meaningful. Something that would make her feel good about herself and her decision. After thinking about it for a minute or two, though, she couldn't come up with anything that seemed unique enough.

Oh well, Stevie decided after a moment, returning to her task. *I'm sure I'll have plenty of time to think about it tonight while Mom and Dad have me polishing the lightbulbs or vacuuming the ceilings or whatever. I'll just have to make good use of that time and think of something really special.*

Lisa glanced wistfully at the Lakes' house as she drove past it on her way to her own home a couple of doors down. It was almost four o'clock, and she had just gotten out of the monthly meeting of Willow Creek High School's photography club. She felt a pang of longing to spend some time with Alex. It seemed like such a long time since the days when she'd been able to drop by and see him whenever she felt like it.

But that kind of casual visit had been out of the question for the past couple of weeks. Instead, Lisa planned to drop her car off at home, then walk over to Pine Hollow to spend some quality time with Prancer. Thanks to all the time she'd wasted the day before, cooking that not-so-special dinner for her mother, she hadn't had a chance to visit the mare at all.

At least Mom's working the evening shift today, so she'll be on her way to the mall by now, she thought as she hit her turn signal and spun the wheel to take the turn into her driveway. *After that scene last night, I'm not sure I'm ready to face her again.* She still couldn't believe the way her mother had reacted to her news about college. The two of them had managed to miss each other that morning, since Lisa had left for school

70

before her mother had come downstairs for breakfast. And with Mrs. Atwood's work schedule, Lisa was hoping she could put off their next talk about college until the next day or maybe even the day after that.

Just then Lisa's gaze fell on the white sedan parked in front of the garage. Her mother's car.

Lisa gulped. "What's she doing home?" she muttered. For a second she was tempted to back out of the driveway again and speed off to Pine Hollow before her mother saw her.

But then she shook her head. *Don't be ridiculous*, she chided herself, parking her car beside her mother's. *It's not as if you can avoid her until you go off to college next fall. Anyway, Mom's always been pretty excitable. She reacted without thinking last night, that's all. By now she's probably settled down and thought about it and is just waiting for the chance to tell me that I was right and she was wrong.*

When Lisa entered the house, she found her mother waiting for her in the front hall, her expression unreadable. "Hello, Lisa," Mrs. Atwood said. "I've been waiting for you."

"Um, hi," Lisa replied. "I thought you had to work today."

"I took the day off." Mrs. Atwood gestured toward the kitchen. "Let's sit down for a few minutes and talk, all right?"

71

Lisa glanced at her watch. If she wanted to have time to visit with Prancer this afternoon, she needed to leave soon. "Can we talk at dinner?" she asked. "I have something important to do."

Mrs. Atwood's calm expression faltered, and she frowned. "This can't wait," she said sharply. "Nothing's more important than your future."

Lisa swallowed hard. So much for her hope that her mother might have come around overnight to her way of thinking. "Fine," she said. "So let's go talk."

She followed her mother into the kitchen. Mrs. Atwood took a seat at the table and folded her hands in front of her. "Lisa," she said, "I'm very concerned about this college business."

Lisa sat down across from her. "You shouldn't be," she said. "I know what I'm doing."

Mrs. Atwood shook her head grimly. "I don't think so," she said. "I really don't think you've thought this through."

"I told you." Lisa felt her temper rising, but she made an effort to hold it back. She'd been dealing with her mother for seventeen and a half years. By now she knew that it rarely did much good to get mad at her. "I thought about it a lot. This decision is the best one for me."

"Best for you?" Mrs. Atwood shot back. "Or best for Alex?"

"What?" Lisa blinked, taken by surprise.

Her mother leaned forward. "Did he talk you into this?" she demanded. "Did he convince you that you should stay nearby so that you could stay together?"

"Of course not!" Lisa could hardly believe that her mother could suggest such a thing. "He didn't even know about this until after I did it."

Mrs. Atwood looked unconvinced. "But you *have* thought about it," she said leadingly. "That your boyfriend still has one more year of high school. That it would be easier to stay together if you stayed nearby."

"Well, sure, of course," Lisa said, feeling a little flustered. "But that's certainly not the only—"

"So what did he have to say about that, hmm?" Mrs. Atwood leaned back, staring at her daughter through narrowed eyes. "Has he started making comments about dating other people next year if you're far away from each other? Did he tell you that if you really loved him, you'd be willing to make sacrifices for him?"

"No!" Lisa blinked. "What are you talking about? Alex would never say anything like that. He's not that kind of person."

Mrs. Atwood shook her head, still looking grim. "That's what I used to think about your father," she said bitterly. "Until he came to my dorm one weekend and announced that he needed me to be there for him full-time, and that if I wasn't willing to make that sacrifice, he would have to look around for someone who was." She shrugged. "I made the wrong decision. I decided to drop out and marry him, live with him at his college while he finished his degree. And now, almost thirty years later, look where that decision got me: alone, struggling to support myself and my daughter, stuck in a dead-end job. I don't want that to happen to you, Lisa. You never know what's going to happen when it comes to relationships."

Lisa blinked, shocked by her mother's comments. She knew that her mother hadn't finished college. But she'd had no idea . . .

Mrs. Atwood seemed to take her daughter's momentary silence as some kind of agreement. "It doesn't sound so good when you think about it that way, does it?" she said. "Now are you willing to talk about how we can fix this before it's too late?"

"No!" Lisa exclaimed, startled out of her thoughts about her parents' past. "I'm sorry if you feel like you made the wrong decision, but this is *my* life we're talking about here, not yours," she said hotly. "I'm not you, and Alex isn't Dad. I know what I'm doing."

"You're seventeen years old," Mrs. Atwood replied. "You can't possibly understand the consequences of this."

Lisa leaped out of her chair. "You're the one who doesn't understand!" she cried. "You won't even listen to what I'm trying to tell you! I've thought about this—I've thought about it more than you can possibly know. I'm not making any sacrifices here. NVU gave me a scholarship, which you would know if you hadn't started freaking out before I could tell you that last night. A *good* scholarship. And they want me to join the honors program."

"Of course they do," Mrs. Atwood snapped. "They're no fools. They know they'd be lucky to get a terrific student like you. They know you can take your pick of schools."

Lisa smacked her hands on the table in frustration. She couldn't take this much longer. Why wouldn't her mother shut up and listen, try to understand instead of just insisting that Lisa was ruining her life? "You don't get it," she said. "How can I explain this to you when you won't even listen to me?"

"I don't know," Mrs. Atwood said sourly. "But you'll have to explain it to your father as well. Because I called him this morning, and he's as upset about this as I am."

Lisa was so stunned that she couldn't respond for a moment. As far as she knew, her mother hadn't voluntarily spoken to her father since the divorce. "You called Dad?" she choked out at last. "You actually called him?"

"Believe me, it wasn't pleasant for me," her mother replied with a frown. "But he is still your father, and I knew he would want to know what you were up to."

Lisa wasn't sure she trusted her mother's motives. *She probably still suspected that Dad put me up to this somehow*, she thought irritably. *She probably thought we were sneaking around, scheming behind her back just for the sake of leaving her out.*

"It's no wonder he's upset if you just called to yell about how horrible I am," Lisa snapped. "I think maybe I'd better call him and give him my version. Because I'm sure he'll understand why I'm doing this."

To her surprise, her mother just shrugged and gestured toward the phone. "Be my guest," she said. "Call him."

"I will." Lisa frowned, then walked over to the phone. Glancing at the clock on the microwave oven, she realized that her father would still be at his office.

She dialed his work number, shooting her mother a glance out of the corner of her eye. Mrs. Atwood wasn't looking at her. She was still sitting at the table, staring at her hands. Lisa wasn't sure, but she suspected her mother was staring at the finger where her wedding ring had once been. She had done that a lot right after the divorce, though Lisa hadn't noticed it as much lately.

She was jarred out of her thoughts when a woman's voice answered the phone. Lisa recognized the lilting voice of her father's secretary, Charla. As soon as Lisa identified herself, Charla put her straight through, and a moment later her father came on the line.

"Dad?" Lisa said when she heard his familiar voice, her face relaxing into a smile. "Hi! It's me, Lisa."

"Ah. Hold on a second, Lisa." She heard him speaking to someone else in the room, though she couldn't understand what he said. A moment later, he returned to the line. "I'm sort of in the middle of something here, so I really can't talk for long right now. But I have to know one thing: Was your mother getting all worked up over nothing when she called this morning? Because she claims Northern Virginia accepted you already and you told them you're enrolling there."

"No, that's right, Dad," Lisa said. "I decided I'm going to NVU next year. I got a scholarship and everything. I was going to tell you when I saw you next week. You know, as a surprise."

"This is a surprise, all right." His voice was stern. "I can't believe you actually sent back an acceptance to college already, especially without talking to at least one of us first. I thought you were sensible enough not to pull a stunt like this, Lisa."

"What?" Lisa wasn't sure she had heard him right. Was she mistaken, or did he sound just as disapproving as her mother had? "But Dad—"

He cut her off before she could explain. "Look, like I said, I can't talk now, but we're going to have to discuss this and figure out what to do. Soon."

Lisa couldn't manage a response. A second later, she heard the line go dead as her father hung up the phone.

FIVE

"*Hi, Carole,*" said an unfamiliar girl's voice on the answering machine. The girl sounded eager and confident, the words tumbling over one another in a rush. "*My name's Tanya, Tanya Appel. My friend's brother's girlfriend's friend's cousin Stevie Lake gave me your number—she said you have this really great horse you want to sell. He sounds just perfect for me. I'm looking for a horse who's a good jumper so I can enter shows with him. Stevie says your horse—Starlight, right?—is a terrific jumper and really well trained and everything. So call me back. I'd love to come over as soon as possible and check him out. If I like him, I'm sure we can work out a price really fast. My parents already said I can get pretty much any horse I want.*" The girl went on to give her phone number twice, then repeated her name once again.

With a gulp, Carole jabbed the Erase button on the machine. "Whoa," she muttered. "That was fast." Stevie certainly hadn't wasted any time giving Tanya Carole's phone number. And Tanya had wasted even less time using it.

"Hi, sweetie! I'm home!" Colonel Hanson's voice boomed out at that moment. "Carole? Are you here?"

"I'm in the kitchen, Dad," Carole called, trying to keep her voice steady. She couldn't believe how close she'd come to having her secret blown. What if her father had come home a few minutes earlier and checked the messages before Carole got there? She hadn't breathed a word to him yet about her decision to sell Starlight. It wasn't because she liked keeping secrets from him—since her mother had died years ago, Carole and her father were very close. She shared just about everything important that happened in her life with him, with only a few exceptions. One of those exceptions was that history test, of course—that was one thing she knew she could never tell him about. Not ever.

This was different, though. She would tell him about Starlight soon. She just wanted to have something concrete to share with him first, so he would realize how serious she was about this. So he would see how responsible and mature she was being. Of course, he probably wouldn't have thought she was too responsible and mature if he'd come across that phone message with no warning.

It's my fault, Carole thought. *I should have reminded Stevie to tell that girl not to leave an incriminating message.*

Colonel Hanson strode into the room, pausing just long enough to give Carole a quick kiss on top of her head as he passed. Heading straight for the refrigerator, he grabbed a carton of orange juice and poured himself a glass.

"Whew!" he exclaimed. "I'm beat. This rat race is brutal after all those nice, relaxing years in the Marines."

Carole smiled. Her father had recently retired from military life and now had a thriving second career giving motivational speeches at conferences and business retreats all over the country. He was also a prominent member of several important charity boards, which meant that he sometimes put in long hours at all sorts of glamorous parties and fund-raisers.

"It's a tough life, Dad, but someone has to do it." Carole willed herself not to so much as glance at the answering machine. "What was it tonight—dinner and dancing? Or just drinks with the President and Secretary of State?"

"Neither." Colonel Hanson gulped down his juice and smiled at her. "Just going over some paperwork with the Bonner Foundation's lawyers. Boring stuff. No horses involved at all."

"Bummer," Carole said. "So should we order a pizza or something? Sounds like we're both too wiped out to cook tonight."

Colonel Hanson loosened his shirt collar. "You go ahead if you want. I already ate." At Carole's suspicious glance, he smiled sheepishly. "Okay, okay, you caught me. The lawyers and I actually went over that paperwork at a really nice Japanese restaurant in D.C."

"So when you were complaining about the rat race a minute ago, what you really meant was the sushi race," Carole joked weakly. She was itching to get to the phone and call Tanya back. The girl had sounded awfully eager, and Carole didn't want her to get impatient and call back again.

Colonel Hanson set his empty juice glass in the sink and yawned. "Well, using those chopsticks can be exhausting," he said. "I realize it's kind of early, but you know what they say about early to bed, early to rise. I'm going to hit the shower and then hit the sack."

"Okay. See you in the morning." Carole waited until her father's footsteps moved up the stairs and she heard the shower turn on overhead; then she grabbed the phone and punched in Tanya Appel's number. Moments later, it was all settled. Tanya was coming to Pine Hollow to see Starlight the very next day.

Callie was brushing her teeth when the phone rang that night at eleven-twenty. She didn't pay much attention at first—her congressman father's home district was on the West Coast, the time zone three hours earlier. It wasn't unusual for him to get calls as late as midnight from staff members or constituents back home, even on weekdays.

But a moment later, there was a knock on the bathroom door. "Callie?" her mother called. "Are you in there? It's for you."

Callie spit out a mouthful of toothpaste. "Just a sec," she called, surprised. Scanning her mental list of friends from her old hometown who might be calling, she hurriedly rinsed out her mouth and grabbed her crutches.

Mrs. Forester was standing in the hall when Callie emerged from the bathroom. She held out the cordless phone. "Don't talk long, sweetheart," she said in a gently disapproving tone. "It's getting late."

"Okay." Callie took the phone and swung into her bedroom on her crutches. "Hello?"

"Callie?" George Wheeler's familiar, slightly high-pitched voice greeted her from the other end of the line. "Hi, it's me."

Callie frowned. "George?" She glanced at her watch. "Uh, hi. What is it?"

"Sorry for calling so late," George said, "but I was just feeling really worried about you, and I thought I should check in on you."

"Worried?" Callie repeated. She sat down on the edge of her bed, dropped her crutches on the rug, and switched the phone to her other ear. "About me? Why?"

"Well, I noticed you haven't been to Pine Hollow in two days," George replied. "I know you usually do your therapeutic riding every day, so I was afraid something might be wrong that you weren't telling me about."

Callie shook her head, wondering if she was missing something here. George sounded really concerned. "Uh, no, nothing's wrong," she told him. "I had a doctor's appointment yesterday, and then today I had plans with my family."

Not that it's any of your business, she thought uncomfortably. *Besides, if you were so worried about me, why didn't you just wait to ask me about this in school tomorrow? It's not like we don't sit right next to each other all through chemistry class. It's not like we don't run into each other a million times every day at school.*

"Whew!" George exclaimed. "Well, that explains it. I was just afraid that maybe—well, never mind. So you'll be there tomorrow?"

"Sure," Callie replied. "But listen, I should go now. It's kind of late, and I was just on my way to bed."

George laughed sheepishly. "Okay, sorry about that," he said. "I wouldn't normally call so late. I hope your folks aren't mad."

"Don't worry about it," Callie reassured him, trying to sound cheerful. "I'll see you tomorrow at school, okay?"

"Okay. Good night, Callie."

Callie hit the button to hang up and then sat there for a moment, staring at the phone in her hand. *What was that all about?* she wondered. *And how did I get myself into this weird friendship with George, anyway?*

Before she could come up with an answer to that, her brother poked his head into her room. "Who was that?" he asked curiously.

"George Wheeler," Callie replied, setting the phone on her bedside table. "He was freaking out because he hasn't seen me at the stable for a couple of days."

Scott's handsome face scrunched into a puzzled frown. "Huh?"

"Yeah, that's about how I feel," Callie admitted. She sighed and leaned back against her pillow. "I know George and I are just friends now, but I still get a weird vibe from him sometimes. I

85

feel kind of bad about being so touchy when he means well, but—"

"Get a clue, Callie." Scott stepped into her room and leaned against her bedpost, looking down at her seriously. "I don't care what George says about being friends. The guy obviously still has a totally desperate crush on you. It's written all over him. And it's not like you to put up with that kind of situation."

Callie shook her head quickly. "No, that's not what's happening here," she insisted. "We really are just friends. I mean, George hardly even seemed upset when I told him I didn't like him in any other way."

Scott snorted and folded his arms across his chest. "Uh-huh," he said sarcastically. "And he had only the purest motives when he decided to call you at eleven-thirty at night just to check up on what you've been doing lately. Get real."

Callie pursed her lips. She had to admit that her brother had a point. "Hmmm," she said, thinking back over George's behavior. How much had it really changed since their one disastrous date? He talked a lot about how they were friends now. Otherwise, he still acted just about the same. He turned up to walk her to class whenever his schedule allowed, he stopped by to watch her therapeutic riding sessions at Pine Hollow at least a few times a week, he hung on her every word. . . . "Okay, maybe you have a point," she said. "But I already told George where we stand. In no uncertain terms. He says he wants to be friends, so what more can I do about it?"

Scott shrugged. "There's nothing that says you have to be friends with him," he pointed out. "You could just blow him off." He smiled slightly. "I've seen you do that to guys before. And most of them never bothered you again, right?"

"That's different." Callie thought back to some of the obnoxious guys who'd pursued her back in her old hometown. She'd never felt a moment's hesitation about telling them off when they got too aggressive. But George wasn't like those guys. He was so sensitive, so vulnerable. "I don't want to hurt his feelings," she told Scott. "Like I said, he knows how things stand. I'm sure he'll adjust sooner or later." She shoved her feet under the bedcovers and yawned, suddenly feeling very tired. "I just have to give him a little more time to let it all sink in."

SIX

"Carole!" Denise McCaskill called as Carole hurried down the aisle with a wheelbarrow full of soiled bedding. "Do you know where the chain shank is? I can't find it anywhere, and the farrier won't go near Geronimo without it."

Carole skidded to a stop, almost upending the wheelbarrow in the process. "I'm not sure," she told Max's petite young stable manager, trying to recall her last glimpse of the piece of equipment Denise needed. "The last place I saw it was hanging on that hook outside the wash stall. Did you check there?"

Denise shook her head. "Thanks," she called over her shoulder as she turned and raced back down the aisle and around the corner.

Carole got her wheelbarrow moving again, continuing toward the back door and the dirt path leading to the manure pit. It was already almost four o'clock, and she was feeling a little frantic. It didn't help that the rest of the staff was in the same kind of mood. Everyone seemed to have a million things to do before it was time to leave for the big show, now just three days away.

Or in my case, a million and one things, Carole thought as she reached the manure pit and tilted her wheelbarrow, dumping its contents onto the pile. *In addition to everything else, I have to find time to show off Starlight to that girl.*

As she turned and steered the wheelbarrow back toward the stable building, she checked her watch. Starlight's potential buyer, Tanya Appel, was due to arrive at Pine Hollow in a little more than half an hour.

Okay, Carole thought as she stowed the wheelbarrow in the equipment stall and brushed off her hands. *Half an hour. That should give me just enough time to bring Prancer in from the meadow and walk her for twenty minutes or so, and then maybe check in with the farrier about the new mare's shoeing schedule before Tanya gets here. And if she's late, it probably wouldn't hurt to run out back and give Starlight a quick grooming, just to make sure he's looking his best.*

She hurried toward the stable office. As she entered, she caught a glimpse through the window of an unfamiliar car pulling to a stop in the parking area. A red-haired girl was sitting in the front seat, staring out the window with an eager expression on her freckled face.

Carole gulped. She was pretty certain that this stranger was Tanya Appel. *"You'll be able to recognize me right away,"* she'd announced to Carole on the phone the night before. *"My hair's almost as red as my name. Appel, get it?"*

Carole raced out of the office and down the hallway to the stable entrance, arriving just in time to intercept the red-haired girl. She definitely didn't want Max or Red or Denise to find the newcomer and ask her what she was doing there. "Hi! I'm Carole Hanson," she said, thanking her lucky stars that she'd glanced out the window at just the right moment. "Are you—"

"Hi, Carole! I'm Tanya," the girl said brightly. "Sorry I'm kind of early, but I just couldn't wait to get here." Her voice was high-pitched and rather loud, but cheerful and friendly. She gestured at a thin auburn-haired woman who was trailing along behind her. The woman was wearing large, round eyeglasses, which gave her an owlish look. "This is my mom," Tanya said. "She drove me here."

Carole smiled politely at the woman. "How do you—"

"So where is he?" Tanya demanded with a grin, hopping impatiently from one foot to the other. "Starlight, I mean. I can't wait to see him! I had a dream last night—I was riding this awesome bay horse, he had a gorgeous mahogany

90

coat and a big white blaze, and he was so amazing and nice and sweet and smart and talented that I just knew he was the horse for me."

"Well," Carole said, a little taken aback by Tanya's rapid-fire chatter. "Starlight has a star on his forehead, not a blaze. But otherwise the horse in your dream sounds a lot like—"

"I've always loved bays," Tanya said eagerly. "They're just so beautiful, you know?"

Carole nodded. "Well, sure," she agreed. "Though of course a horse's color isn't really—"

"Hey, why are we standing around here when we could be checking out Starlight right this minute?" Tanya asked. "Let's have less talking and more walking. Where's his stall?"

"Actually, I already turned him out in our back paddock," Carole explained. "I thought it would be easier for us to—"

"Whatever," Tanya broke in. "So lead the way."

Carole just nodded and gestured for Tanya and her mother to follow as she headed for the back door. She felt a bit overwhelmed by Tanya's enthusiasm. Still, she was sure that most of the girl's impatience was due to excitement. She couldn't blame her for that. Getting your own horse was a wonderful thing, something most people dreamed about and planned for and anticipated for a long time. She also knew that it didn't pay to jump into this kind of decision too fast or let your emotions take over. Just about every horse had his wonderful points and his not-so-great ones. A potential owner had to figure out what she wanted and needed from her new mount and carefully decide if each horse she saw met those criteria. She also had to ride the horse and have a vet examine it for health and soundness. Only then could she really know if a particular horse was truly the horse of her dreams.

She and the Appels had just reached the back door when Carole heard Max calling her name. "Excuse me for a second, okay?" she told the visitors hurriedly. "Starlight's in the little paddock just out there to the right. Why don't you go take a look at him, and I'll be back to introduce you in a minute."

Tanya nodded and rushed for the door, dragging her mother behind her. As soon as they were safely out of sight, Carole turned and raced back up the aisle, almost running into Max as he hurried around the corner toward her.

"Oh, there you are," Max said as Carole skidded to a stop in front of him. "Where were you?"

"Um, I was just, uh . . . ," Carole began.

"Never mind." Max waved one hand, looking frazzled. "Did you have a chance to bring

Prancer in yet? Because Judy's going to stop by in a little while to look at Patch's foot, and she said she'd like to take a quick look at Prancer if she's in her stall."

"Not yet," Carole admitted. "Um, I'll get her soon, okay? When's Judy supposed to get here?"

Max checked his watch. "Not sure," he said. "It'll be at least an hour. She was going to swing by Hedgerow Farms and then head over here after that."

"Okay. I'll make sure Prancer's in her stall by then," Carole promised.

Max nodded and hurried on his way, and Carole heaved a sigh of relief. Now maybe she could get back to her visitors.

As she headed for the back door once again, she caught a glimpse of Ben walking in through it, leading a school horse named Chippewa. Carole felt a moment of panic—she couldn't afford to have anyone see Tanya out there with Starlight and figure out what was going on, and Ben must have walked right past the back paddock. But then she relaxed. She had never actually come right out and told Ben that she'd decided to sell her horse, but she was sure he'd already guessed. So far he had kept his mouth shut about it, not even hinting at the topic to Carole herself. She knew he was the last person who would go blabbing to Max about Tanya's visit.

"Hi," Carole said. "Um, I was just on my way out back to, um—" She winced as she heard a shriek of delight from outside that could only be Tanya.

Ben's dark eyes flicked toward the back entrance, then returned to Carole's face. "Right," he said. "Uh, I'd better . . . you know." He gestured at Chip and made a move as if to walk on.

At that moment Carole caught a glimpse of movement as someone turned the corner at the end of the aisle. Looking up, she saw Maxi coming toward them. "Hi, Carole!" the little girl sang out eagerly when she spotted them, picking up her pace.

"Hi, Maxi." Carole smiled back, trying not to let her nervousness show. Since when did so many people congregate in this back arm of the stable loop? Then she realized that she and Ben were standing right in front of Krona's stall and guessed that Max's daughter was coming to visit her pony. "What are you up to today?"

"I'm waiting for Callie." Maxi played with the end of one reddish braid. "She's going to take me for a ride. She said she would get here at, um, four o'clock."

Carole glanced at her watch, feeling frazzled. She didn't have the energy or the patience to deal with Maxi at the moment. "It's not four

94

yet," she said briskly. "You still have ten minutes until she's supposed to get here. So why don't you go wait for her out front, okay?"

The little girl shrugged. "That's okay. She said she'd find me," she explained. She smiled at Carole hopefully. "I can help with your chores if you want. For ten minutes, I mean."

Carole gulped, wondering how to get rid of Maxi without being unkind. "Oh, thanks," she said slowly. "That's really nice of you. But, um . . ." She searched her mind frantically, trying to come up with an excuse.

Ben shot Carole a keen glance, then quickly moved his gaze over his shoulder to the back door. He cleared his throat and turned to face the little girl. "Uh, listen, Maxi," he said gruffly. "I was just going to groom Chip here." He gave the steady Appaloosa, who was standing patiently at his side, a hearty pat. "How about if you, you know, help me?"

Maxi cocked a suspicious eye at him. Carole almost smiled as she realized that this might very well be the first time the taciturn young stable hand had ever spoken directly to the little girl.

"Go ahead, Maxi," Carole said in an encouraging tone. "I'm sure Ben could really use your help."

"Okay," Maxi agreed, still sounding uncertain. "I guess I can help him. Only for ten minutes, though."

She followed the stable hand down the aisle, her suspicion gone, chattering at him about everything she knew about grooming. Carole sent a silent prayer of thanks after Ben. Finally she was free to return to Tanya. She would have to remember to tell Ben later how much she appreciated what he'd done.

She rushed out to the back paddock, arriving breathlessly beside Mrs. Appel just in time to see Tanya walk up to Starlight, who was standing calmly in the middle of the paddock, and pat him on the neck. Carole saw immediately what had happened. Tanya had been so excited to meet Starlight that she hadn't bothered to wait for Carole's return before letting herself into the paddock with the horse.

Carole almost shouted out for the younger girl to get back. It was very foolish to approach a horse you didn't know that way, even if someone had assured you that the horse was gentle. Horses could be unpredictable, and it was hard to tell what might set them off. If Starlight had been a kicker or had had an unreliable temperament, Tanya could have been putting herself in danger of injury or worse.

But Carole forced herself to swallow her reprimand. After all, in this case it didn't really matter if Tanya had acted carelessly. Starlight was an easygoing horse, with no dangerous vices or fear of friendly strangers. Maybe Carole would say something to her later, just to make sure she understood how risky her behavior could be in a different situation. But she didn't want to ruin the younger girl's excited mood right then.

"So what do you think of him?" she called, letting herself into the paddock.

Tanya turned to her with a bright smile. "He's wonderful!" she exclaimed, running her hand down Starlight's neck. "So friendly and gentle!"

Lucky for you, Carole thought grimly. But she forced herself to return the other girl's smile. The important thing here was that Tanya seemed impressed.

"He really is a sweetheart," Carole said. "He has a very steady temperament. I don't think he's ever put his ears back at me except when the vet was giving him a shot." She shrugged. "He hates needles, but who can blame him for that, right?"

Tanya didn't appear to be listening to Carole. She was too busy running her hands over Starlight's smooth bay coat. "He's gorgeous," she breathed. "It looks like he might even be a Thoroughbred. Is he?"

"He's got some Thoroughbred in him," Carole replied. "But he's not a purebred, no."

"Oh." Tanya shrugged. "Well, anyway, he's really beautiful."

"Thanks. Do you want to tack him up and try him out?" Carole knew that a lot of prospective horse owners preferred to tack up each prospect themselves to make sure that the horse was easy to handle. So instead of getting Starlight ready before Tanya's arrival, Carole had just brought out his saddle and bridle and hung them on the fence post nearby. She had also brought out a longe line in case Tanya wanted to use that.

"Sure." Tanya took Starlight by the halter and led him toward the tack on the fence. The bay gelding followed obediently, then stood quietly while Tanya picked up a lead rope and clipped it to his halter.

Carole walked over to offer help if needed, but Tanya didn't seem to expect her assistance. Watching the younger girl critically, Carole saw that Tanya definitely knew what she was doing. She fastened Starlight's lead line to the fence to keep him still, then positioned the saddle pad and saddle on the gelding's broad, smooth back, talking soothingly to him the whole time. She brought the girth down carefully, not simply tossing it over the horse's side as many inexperienced riders did. In a matter of moments, she had the girth fastened securely and had pulled each of Starlight's forelegs forward to ensure that

98

his skin wasn't wrinkled beneath it. Then she picked up the bridle with the same easy confidence and started putting it on.

Carole felt herself relax slightly. She wouldn't know for sure until she saw Tanya ride, of course, but she already had the feeling that this girl was more than proficient enough to handle Starlight. He was a good, obedient horse, but he was too strong and frisky for a beginner. He required a rider who knew what she was doing, and so far it seemed that Tanya fit the bill.

So what if she's a little loud, a little impulsive? Carole said to herself as she watched the younger girl bring the bridle's crown piece up over Starlight's ears, being careful not to catch his forelock under the browband. *So what if she doesn't always seem to listen to what I'm saying? She's probably just excited. She definitely seems to like Starlight so far. And I'm sure she'll like him even more once she puts him through his paces.*

When Starlight was ready, Tanya swung into the saddle, not even waiting for Carole to give her a leg up. Once again, Carole was impressed with the younger girl's assurance. Tanya sat confidently in the saddle, her back straight and her hands and legs in almost perfect position. After leaning over long enough to adjust her stirrups, she glanced over and tossed Carole a grin. "Here we go!" she sang out before signaling for a walk.

Starlight stepped off dutifully, and after a moment Tanya urged him into a trot. Once again, Starlight responded immediately.

Carole smiled, feeling her heart swell with pride. Her horse had really come a long way since their early days together. He had been young and pretty green when she'd gotten him, but her hard work and his willing disposition had combined to turn him into a beautifully trained riding horse.

"Wow!" Tanya called as she and Starlight came around the paddock past Carole. "His trot is amazing. It's so smooth you really don't even want to post!"

Carole gave her a thumbs-up without responding, since they were already almost past her. She was glad that Tanya appreciated Starlight's trot. It had always been one of Carole's favorite things about him, too.

See? Carole told herself. *Tanya's a terrific rider. Starlight is really responding to her. Does it matter if she seems . . . well, maybe just a little too sure of herself? He wouldn't let her get away with it if she didn't actually know what she was doing in the saddle. And that's really all that matters, right?*

Just then Carole happened to glance over at Tanya's mother. Mrs. Appel had been so quiet since arriving that Carole had almost forgotten she was there.

"Your daughter must have been taking lessons for a long time," Carole commented politely, smiling at the woman. "She's very good."

Mrs. Appel blinked at Carole behind her glasses. "Oh, yes," she said in a soft, almost whispery voice. "My Tanya can do anything she sets her mind to."

After a few more turns around the small ring, Tanya glanced over at Carole. "I'm going to try taking him over the jumps now, okay?" she called.

Carole nodded. She had set up a couple of small obstacles in the paddock for that very purpose, knowing that if Tanya was really interested in Starlight, she would want to test his jumping ability. She had mentioned on the phone that she was looking for a good jumper, and Starlight was definitely that. He might not be quite up to the competition at a show like Colesford, but he had more than enough talent to win a truckful of ribbons with a good junior rider like Tanya.

Carole watched as Tanya rode toward the first low fence at a trot, her expression intent and eager as she took its measure. As Starlight took off, Tanya's hands slid forward and her seat lifted slightly out of the saddle. The gelding sailed over the jump easily, landing cleanly on the other side, and Tanya settled just as easily into the impact. She immediately aimed the horse toward the next fence, shortening his stride slightly to adjust for his speed on the approach. Once again, the pair jumped cleanly and easily.

Seeing the horse jump reminded Carole of Saturday's show, and her mind drifted as she reviewed the last-minute exercises she'd mapped out for Samson. She wanted to have him as sharp as possible on the big day. They would both have to be in tip-top condition if they wanted to make a good showing against the accomplished riders who would be competing against them in Open Jumping. . . .

"I'm sold!" Tanya exclaimed, jerking Carole out of her thoughts as she pulled Starlight up in front of her. "I totally love him!"

"That's great," Carole replied. "Um, but are you sure? I mean, I'm sure you want to think about it. You're welcome to come back and see him again in a few days if you like. Maybe next week would be best, because this weekend I'll be—"

"That's okay," Tanya interrupted. "I always make up my mind quickly. And I've definitely decided Starlight is awesome."

"Don't forget, dear," Mrs. Appel said, sounding rather tentative, "your father said you should make sure to have Dr. Sarver see the horse first."

Tanya rolled her eyes. "No duh, Mother," she

said. "I know how these things work better than you do, remember?"

Mrs. Appel shrugged and smiled appeasingly. "I know, I'm sorry," she said. "It's just that you seem so excited, I just wanted—"

"Okay, then," Tanya cut her off before turning back to Carole. "So I'll call you after I talk to my vet, all right?"

Carole smiled uncertainly. "All right." Remembering the close call with the answering machine, she added, "But could you only call me in the evening? I'm usually here all afternoon—you can reach me at home between nine and eleven o'clock." *And I'll just have to make sure to be there during that time so that I can grab the phone before Dad does*, she added to herself.

"Whatever." Tanya glanced over at Starlight and smiled. "Bye, handsome!" she called to the horse, blowing him a kiss. "I'll see you real soon!" After another good-bye for Carole, she left, her mother hurrying along in her wake.

When they were gone, Carole let herself back into the paddock and walked over to Starlight. "You did a good job, boy," she whispered, taking hold of his bridle. "She really loved you."

Starlight snorted lightly and nudged at her shoulder, obviously hoping for treats. Carole wished she'd thought to bring some. Instead, she scratched him in all his favorite places before leading him inside to his stall.

As she quickly untacked him, Carole thought back over Tanya's visit. She wasn't quite sure what to make of the red-haired girl—she was so loud, so brash and confident. Too confident, maybe. Over the years, Carole had learned that it was usually best to go with your gut when it came to horses, and right then her gut was telling her that Tanya might not be cut out for horse ownership, at least not when the horse in question was Starlight. But Carole didn't quite trust her own instincts in this case. She wasn't sure whether her doubts were based on anything real or were just coming from her own mixed feelings about parting with her beloved horse.

In any case, she decided to try not to worry about it anymore until she heard from Tanya again. After all, just because she'd clearly enjoyed meeting Starlight and claimed he was the one she wanted, that didn't mean she was definitely going to buy him. Once she calmed down and had a chance to think it over, the girl might decide that Starlight wasn't quite right for her for one reason or another.

As Carole wandered down the aisle, trying to put Tanya Appel out of her mind for the moment and remember everything on her lengthy to-do list, she spotted Rachel Hart walking toward the tack room.

"Rachel!" she called. "Hold up. Do you have a second?"

Rachel turned and smiled at her. "Hi, Carole," she said in her soft, sweet voice. "Sure, what's up?"

Carole gestured for the younger girl to follow her into the stable office, which was empty at the moment. When they were inside, she pushed the door most of the way closed and took a deep breath. "Um, did Stevie say anything to you," she began uncertainly, "about, well, you know—"

"About Starlight?" Rachel said helpfully. She nodded. "She talked to me yesterday." She blinked at Carole shyly. "I can't believe you really want to sell him. He's such a nice horse."

"I know. That's why I want to find him a really great new owner." Carole smiled at Rachel hopefully. "So how about it? Do you think he might be the horse for you?"

Rachel was already shaking her head. "I wish," she said sadly. "After I talked to Stevie, I went right home and asked my parents about getting my own horse for my birthday. But they said they have to think about it." She shrugged. "They're not sure I'm ready for a horse of my own, since I've only been taking lessons for two years."

"Oh." Carole felt her heart sink. "That's too bad. I think you and Starlight could really be good together."

Rachel nodded again, looking almost as disappointed as Carole felt. "Me too," she said. "And I bet I could convince my parents, too. But it might take a while." She shrugged. "I'm sure it won't take you very long to find a ton of people who want to buy him."

"Well, maybe," Carole said, remembering Tanya's enthusiasm. "But I'll keep you posted, just in case. In the meantime, I'd really appreciate it if you could keep this quiet. I haven't told Max yet."

"I won't breathe a word, I swear." Rachel crossed her heart.

Carole thanked her and then watched her hurry on toward the tack room. *Too bad*, she thought. *Rachel would really be the perfect solution. Especially since her favorite Pine Hollow horse until lately was Prancer, and now she won't be able to ride her anymore.*

Suddenly remembering her promise to Max, Carole spun around and headed for the entrance, planning to rush out and retrieve Prancer before returning to her other chores. As she emerged into the stable yard, she saw Max standing at the edge of the main schooling ring, watching as one of his adult students trotted over a row of cavalletti.

Carole hurried to his side. "Judy didn't get here yet, did she?" she called to him breathlessly. "I'm on my way to bring Prancer in right now."

"Never mind that," he said, turning to her. "Judy called. An emergency came up at the other farm, and she probably won't make it over here today after all. So you might as well leave Prancer out for the moment. She could use the fresh air, and we have plenty of other things to do before it's time to bring everyone in for the evening feeding."

Carole nodded, thinking of the three days—two and a half, really—remaining before the Colesford Horse Show, and the million and one tasks that absolutely, positively had to be done before they loaded up the horses on Saturday morning. "That's for sure," she told Max. "So what do you need me to do first?"

"Sorry that took so long," Alex said breathlessly, rushing over to the bleachers at the edge of Fenton Hall's soccer field, where Lisa was perched on the lowest bench. "We were, like, a half hour late getting started because of a student council assembly, and then when it was almost time to quit, Coach decided to have all of us run some extra laps just because a couple of the guys started calling each other names."

Lisa tipped her head up to receive his quick kiss, then glanced down at her watch. "That's okay," she said. "I didn't mind waiting. But we probably don't have time for TD's now if you want to be home on time." She couldn't help feeling a little disappointed that there was so little time left before Alex had to be home. She had been anticipating this date—if you could call it that—all week long.

She had also hoped they might have enough time to stop by Pine Hollow on their way back home to pay Prancer a quick visit. Lisa had never made it over to the stable the day before. After speaking to her father, she'd been forced to sit for what felt like forever and listen to her mother rant and rave about how she was ruining her life. By the time Mrs. Atwood ran out of steam, it was already getting dark. Besides, after her upsetting conversations with her parents, Lisa wasn't in the mood to go anywhere.

Alex collapsed on the bench beside her and peeled off his shin guards. "I think you're right," he agreed. "But that's okay. We can still hang out for a few minutes right here if you want."

Lisa smiled at him. "I want."

"Good." Alex grinned at her, then leaned over for another kiss.

After a moment or two Lisa gently pushed him away. "Enough," she said. "We don't have much time, and I want to hear what's new with you. Have your parents decided how long you're grounded for yet?"

"Nope. They still won't say. So basically, the only thing new with me is the calluses on my hands from shoving that stupid vacuum all over the house. What's new with *you*?" Alex grabbed her arm and squeezed it fondly. "I can't believe I haven't even talked to you since the weekend."

Lisa had a hard time believing that herself. It seemed like she spent a whole lot more time figuring out when she might be able to see her boyfriend these days than she did actually seeing him. It was a good thing she saw Stevie at the stable, or she might not even know Alex's soccer schedule. "Well, I guess my only major news is that I told Mom about my college plans the other night like I planned." Lisa shook her head grimly as she remembered that conversation and the one that had followed. "She didn't take it very well. Neither did Dad, actually."

"Really? What did they say?"

Lisa sighed and leaned against his shoulder, appreciating the feeling of his warm body through his T-shirt. "Let's see, where do I start?" She slipped her arm around his waist, not minding that his shirt was slightly damp with sweat.

"They said I should have talked to them before I mailed back that form. That I made my decision too fast and for all the wrong reasons. And basically, that I'm doomed to a life of poverty and woe."

She expected Alex to leap to her defense and try to make her feel better. Instead he was quiet for a few seconds. "Well, obviously that poverty-and-woe one is bogus," he said at last. "But I guess maybe you can't totally blame them for the other stuff."

Surprised, Lisa turned and looked into his face, searching his eyes with her own. "What are you saying?" she asked tentatively. "You almost sound like you agree with them."

Alex shrugged, looking troubled. "I don't know, Lisa," he said. "At first I thought this whole idea of yours was totally great. I mean, I love the idea that we could still see each other every weekend." He took one of her hands in both of his own, stroking her palm with his thumbs. "But maybe it wouldn't have hurt for you to have waited a little longer to make up your mind. You know, checked out some of those other schools you were thinking about a little more. Talked this whole business over with your parents or whoever."

Lisa couldn't believe her ears. "What is this?" she exclaimed, yanking her hand away. "I can't believe *you* don't think I'm capable of making this decision, either!"

"It's not that," Alex insisted quickly. "It's just, this could affect your whole life, you know? I'd hate to end up feeling responsible if later on you decide you made the wrong choice."

"What are you talking about? Why would you feel responsible?"

"You know." Alex blinked at her, still looking worried. "If you chose NVU because of our relationship."

"Is that really what you think?" Lisa cried. "You think *you're* the whole reason—the *only* reason—I decided to go there?"

Alex held up his hands. "I'm just saying—"

"I know what you're saying," Lisa said defensively. "You're saying the same thing Mom and Dad said. That I made a stupid decision for a stupid reason. Well, guess what? I'm not as stupid as you all seem to think. I put a lot of thought into this, and I took a lot of things into consideration. Even some things that didn't have anything at all to do with you."

She jumped up and stormed toward the parking lot before he could answer. *I never would have thought Alex would turn against me, too*, she thought. *But it doesn't matter. It's my life, and I'm the only one who can decide what's right for me. Why can't anyone understand that?*

111

SEVEN

When Callie arrived at Patch's stall at a few minutes after four, she found Max standing there, staring thoughtfully at the pinto gelding. Patch stared back placidly, his jaws moving steadily as he chewed a mouthful of hay.

"Hi," Callie greeted Max. "Is it okay if I take Patch out? I promised Maxi I'd go for a ride with her today. I thought we could ride around the back paddock if it's free."

"The paddock's free as far as I know. But you'd better not take out Patch," Max said thoughtfully. "It looks like he may have bruised his sole slightly when Justine took him out on the trail today. I want Judy to take a look before anyone else rides him."

"Oh." Callie was disappointed. "Well, that's okay. I can help Maxi on foot, like I did last time."

"I have a better idea." Max gave Callie an

appraising look. "What would you think of taking out Windsor instead?"

Callie brightened and shot Max a quick glance to assure herself that he was serious. Windsor was a calm, well-mannered school horse. He wasn't exactly a bucking bronco or even the kind of spirited, headstrong horse that Callie had been accustomed to riding before her accident, but at least he was a little more lively than steady old Patch. "Sure," she told Max eagerly. "I think I'm up for that." She was pleased that Max thought she was ready to take on a new challenge. She had noticed him stopping by to watch her therapeutic riding sessions lately. And she knew that her strength and control were really improving these days—she could almost feel her body regaining more of its misplaced abilities with every passing day. It was nice to know that someone else had noticed how much she was progressing.

Callie hurried to Windsor's stall and soon had the big bay gelding tacked up. A few minutes later she was in the secluded back paddock with Maxi, who was mounted on Krona. The little girl's mood was even more ebullient than usual, and Callie couldn't help being pleased and slightly flattered to think that it probably had something to do with their riding date. Callie had mostly agreed to spend time with Maxi that day because she'd thought it would be a nice thing to do for Max and Deborah, as well as a nice change of pace in her own riding. But now she realized she was glad to see Maxi for her own sake, too.

"Ready to ride?" Callie asked Maxi cheerfully.

"Ready, Freddie!" Maxi replied with a giggle. "What are we going to do today?"

Callie paused to think about that for a moment, keeping a steady hand on Windsor's reins. The gelding hadn't given her any trouble so far, and Callie planned to keep it that way. Windsor was a popular Pine Hollow school horse because of his good manners, his impressive size, and his calm personality. But he could be stubborn sometimes, putting him off-limits to beginning riders. Callie was no beginner, though, and she knew she could handle him. Windsor seemed to know it, too. He stood quietly, flicking his ears back and forth and awaiting orders.

"How about this?" Callie said to Maxi. "We could practice turning first. How does that sound? Do you know the right way to get your pony to turn when you want him to?"

Maxi nodded eagerly. "First I'm supposed to look the way I want Krona to go," she said. "Then I turn myself a little bit, like this." She demonstrated, causing Krona to swing his head to the side. "And I slide my outside leg back and, um, loosen the other hand. Right?"

Callie nodded, satisfied with the answer. She'd known that Maxi knew how to turn, but she knew that it was good to repeat early lessons a lot, especially with such a young student. Callie remembered her own riding instructor teaching her the same sorts of things back when she was just a couple of years older than Maxi.

They went on to other lessons, and Callie found herself having even more fun than she'd had on Sunday. She also found herself impressed, just as she'd been then, with how well the little girl rode. Most kids didn't have the coordination, physical or mental, to start riding until they were seven or so. But at age five, Maxi already had a better seat than a lot of the intermediate riders at Pine Hollow. Her arms were relaxed but steady, and her feet in their tiny boots were positioned correctly in the stirrups. True, she could be impulsive and sometimes careless, but that was only to be expected when you considered a five-year-old's limited attention span.

If she keeps it up, she's going to be incredible when she gets a little older, Callie thought, admiring Maxi's control as she asked Krona to start walking, then stop, then start again. The shaggy

little pony obeyed every command without protest. *I guess that's to be expected from Max's kid.*

Half an hour later they were still at it. It was
partly cloudy—the storm system that had
dumped all that rain on them earlier in the week
still hadn't completely cleared out—but it was
mild for November, and Callie was having a
good time being outside and an even better time
riding Windsor. The bay gelding was a good two
hands taller than Patch, giving Callie a new perspective on the world. He was reliable and usually sedate as long as his rider stayed in control,
but he wasn't a push-button horse like Patch.
Callie knew she couldn't afford to ignore him,
and she was enjoying the feeling of really *riding*
again rather than just going for a ride.

"Okay, Maxi," she called. "Let's do some gait
changes now. I'll call out a gait, then you count
to three and then ask Krona for that gait. Okay?"

A few minutes later, Callie had just called for
a halt and then a trot when she heard the sound
of hoofbeats approaching. Glancing over her
shoulder, she saw George entering the paddock
on his horse, a sleek, talented Trakehner mare
named Joyride.

"Hold on a second, Maxi," Callie called, feeling a flash of annoyance as she realized that
George was riding straight toward them. "Keep
him at a halt, okay?"

"Callie!" George exclaimed, beaming as he urged Joyride toward the paddock gate. "What are you doing here? I didn't even know you were at the stable."

Callie glanced at Maxi, who had pulled Krona up and turned to see who was coming. She wasn't sure, but she thought she caught the little girl wrinkling her nose in distaste before returning her attention to her pony.

"Uh, hi, George," Callie said. "Maxi and I were just taking a ride. What are you doing here?"

George grinned. "Oh, I just happened to be in the neighborhood. When I saw you out here, I figured I'd stop in and say hi." Taking both reins in one hand, he lifted the other and waggled his fingers in her direction. "Hi!"

With some effort, Callie held back a snort. George could be pretty nerdy sometimes. "Okay then," she said lightly. "Um, was there anything else? Because I'm a little busy right now, you know. . . ." She gestured toward Maxi.

George barely glanced at the girl and pony across the paddock. "So how's the therapeutic riding going? Do the doctors know when you're going to be able to get rid of your crutches?"

Which part of "I'm busy" didn't he understand? Callie wondered. She opened her mouth to repeat herself, but Maxi spoke before she could.

"Callie!" the little girl called sharply. "Aren't you going to watch me trot now?"

George started, and Joyride skittered away from the sound of the little girl's shrill voice. George had to remain silent for a moment and return his full attention to his mount, talking to her and using all his aids to remind her that he was in charge. It only took a few seconds for him to bring her back under control, but once the mare was standing quietly again, her rider looked flushed and a little sheepish.

"Sorry about that," George said. "She's feeling pretty fresh today."

"Looks like she could use some exercise," Callie said, trying to sound tactful. "Maybe you ought to take her for a good long hack. You don't want her to get too tight so close to a big show."

"Good idea." Still George lingered, keeping Joyride standing under a tight rein, even though it was clear that the athletic mare was bursting to get moving.

Callie wasn't sure what George was expecting her to say or do next. He just sat there smiling brightly at her. She didn't want to say anything in front of Maxi, but she was starting to feel irritated with his behavior. Friends weren't supposed to make other friends feel awkward and impatient whenever they turned up, were they?

"So did you want something else?" she asked him after a long moment of silence.

George shrugged and smiled. "Nope. Like I said, I just happened to be riding by. When I saw you, I figured I'd stop by and say hi."

"Okay." Callie said briskly. "Well, I guess you probably need to get back to work, huh? So I'll see you later." She urged Windsor into a turn and rode over to Maxi without waiting for an answer. After carefully keeping her eyes on the little girl for a few minutes, Callie finally risked a glance over her shoulder. She was just in time to see George riding away.

Whew, she thought ruefully, feeling relieved. *That was kind of bizarre. If this keeps up, I may have to speak to George again about the meaning of "just friends."*

Forty minutes later, Callie was emerging from Windsor's stall after giving him a good grooming when Red O'Malley called to her from farther down the aisle. "Did George find you?" the stable hand asked, hurrying toward her with a water bucket in each hand.

"What?" Callie asked, not understanding for a moment. Why was George looking for her now?

Red looked distracted. "George Wheeler. He was looking for you earlier. Seemed pretty important. So I told him I thought you were out back with Maxi. Did he find you?"

Then Callie understood. *Right. Just in the neighborhood, huh?* she thought.

"Yeah," she told Red, carefully keeping her voice calm. "He found me."

That settles it, Callie told herself as Red nodded and hurried on his way. *I've got to say something to George. Make it clear to him exactly what this "just friends" business is all about.* She nodded to herself firmly. *I'll talk to him tomorrow at school.*

"What's with you?" Stevie asked her twin as he slammed the dishwasher door shut a little harder than necessary. "You've been looking like the grinch who stole Willow Creek ever since you got home from soccer." She and Alex had been cleaning up the kitchen since dinner had ended ten minutes earlier, and so far Alex had barely said a word.

Alex shot her a sour glance. "Oh yeah?" he said. "Well, I'm glad you noticed. Because it's your fault."

"What is?"

"Lisa's mad at me." Alex shrugged. "She came to hang out after practice today, and we ended up getting into a fight about that whole college thing."

Stevie grabbed a dishrag and started wiping crumbs off the kitchen table, casting her brother a curious glance at the same time. "What do you mean? What did you fight about? I thought you loved the whole idea of her going to school so close by."

"I was thinking about what you said," he muttered. "You know, about how I might be partly responsible for pushing her toward NVU?"

"Yeah?" Stevie said. "You didn't say anything to her, did you? I told you it wouldn't do any good."

Alex turned the knob to start the dishwasher cycle, then leaned against the counter and crossed his arms over his chest, glaring at Stevie. "Well, I couldn't just let her ruin her life because of me," he retorted. "I had to say something. I mean, she's always saying she wants us to be completely honest with each other, right?"

"I guess." Stevie finished wiping the table and tossed the rag toward the sink. "So what happened?"

Alex blew out a sigh of frustration. "What happened is she jumped all over me as soon as I tried to tell her what I was worried about. Said I was just like her parents and that I think she's stupid or something; then she ran off without even giving me a chance to say anything else. So much for total honesty, huh?"

Stevie shook her head. "Wow. That doesn't

sound much like Lisa. She's more the discuss-it-to-death type than the rush-off-in-anger type. Usually, anyway."

"Tell me about it. This whole college thing is making her totally weird. She's definitely not acting like her usual calm, rational, totally organized self." Alex bit his lip. "I mean, even the way she mailed off that acceptance thing without telling anyone is pretty out of character, you know?"

Stevie couldn't help agreeing with that, though she didn't say so. She didn't want Alex to get any more worked up about this than he already was. "Well, sort of. But she's still Lisa underneath it all, you know. I'm sure she'll cool down soon, and then she'll realize you were only trying to help." She gave her brother a friendly punch in the arm. "In the meantime, let me help take your mind off it. Carole's birthday is next week, and I need help coming up with a present for her."

Alex snorted. "Big decision there," he said, walking over to the kitchen table and straddling a chair. "Just go over to that tack shop you guys hang out at so much, close your eyes, and point to something."

"I know, I know." Stevie hopped up onto the edge of the kitchen counter and dangled her legs over the side. "Carole's the easiest person in the world to shop for. But that's just the problem. If she likes everything, how do I get her something she's going to think is really special?" She shrugged. "I mean, short of buying Samson from Max and presenting him to her. Somehow I don't think my allowance is going to cover that."

Alex wrinkled his nose. "Yeah. Especially since you still owe me six dollars for that movie I paid for two months ago."

Stevie ignored the reminder. "Samson . . . ," she murmured slowly, thinking about what she had just said. "He's the only thing Carole thinks is totally special these days."

"Earth to Stevie," Alex said, leaning back and resting his elbows on the table. "Even if you saved for a year, you'd still only have enough to buy, like, maybe one of his hooves or something."

"Uh-huh." Stevie pursed her lips thoughtfully. "But that doesn't matter. Carole will figure out a way to buy Samson from Max if it's the last thing she does. No, I'm just thinking that maybe what I should do is get her something extra *for* Samson. You know, like a new halter or something."

"Yeah, that's special." Alex rolled his eyes sarcastically.

Stevie shot him an annoyed glance. "Give me a break. I'm trying to brainstorm here," she said.

"I'm just saying, a gift that's connected with Samson somehow will probably be the most meaningful thing for her right now. Especially since it might help her get over the Starlight thing." Most people still didn't know that Carole was planning to sell her horse, but as Stevie's twin brother and Lisa's boyfriend, Alex was one of the few who was in on the secret.

"Yeah, I guess that's true," Alex said, sounding more serious. He leaned forward and propped his arms on the back of his chair, gazing at Stevie. "But I just don't think a lousy halter is going to say 'Thinking of you in your time of transition,' or whatever, you know? Even for Carole."

Stevie kicked at the cabinet door below her. "You're probably right. So maybe something a little more personal. A grooming bucket with his name on it? A monogrammed saddle pad?"

"Maybe." Alex shrugged. "But that's all such practical stuff, you know? Stuff she'd buy for herself, or that her dad would get her." He tapped his fingers on the back of his chair. "I'm sure she'd appreciate it and all, but if you really want to make it special, do what I did for Lisa's birthday last year."

Stevie smirked. "What, compose a love poem and beg her to make out with me? I don't think so. We're close, but not *that* close."

"Very funny," Alex said. "If you don't shape up, I won't tell you."

"Okay, okay," Stevie said, relenting. "What, O great king of personal shoppers? Please share your brilliant birthday secret with me."

Alex shot her a dirty look, but he complied. "I was going crazy trying to come up with the perfect gift. Lisa and I hadn't been together that long then—just four months or so. I had no idea what I could get her to let her know how much she meant to me. . . ." His voice trailed off and he shot a quick glance at Stevie. "You know. Anyway. So I thought of about a million things that she might like—a leather wallet, some new CDs she'd been wanting, a nice blouse, a fancy lens for her camera, a gift certificate for her favorite bookstore. But I wasn't sure any of those things were special enough. They all seemed like things that just anyone would get her, you know?"

"So what did you end up getting her?" Stevie asked curiously, realizing that she had no idea what her brother had given his girlfriend for her birthday the previous spring.

Alex shrugged. "I sort of gave up on trying to figure it out," he admitted. "I decided to just get her what I wanted to give her instead of worrying so much about what she liked. So I went to

125

the jewelry store at the mall and bought her a necklace with a tiny diamond chip in it."

"You mean that little pendant she always wears?" Stevie raised an eyebrow as what her brother was telling her suddenly clicked into place. "So that's where she got that. I guess I must have assumed her dad gave that to her—I never really thought about it. And she never told us." That last part was a little strange to think about. There had been a time when Lisa, Stevie, and Carole had shared everything about their lives with each other as a matter of course. Still, Stevie reminded herself, she didn't always tell her friends absolutely everything about her relationship with Phil anymore. And she should have realized that Lisa would also have private moments with her boyfriend—moments that she would want to keep private, even from her best friends.

Alex smiled. "She loved it," he said. "And I think part of the reason is that it was totally impractical. It wasn't anything she needed or even particularly wanted before she had it. I mean, she never would have asked for something like that. But maybe that was part of why it worked."

"I see what you mean." Stevie nodded. "But still, Carole isn't Lisa. I really don't think she'd be into it if I got her something totally impractical like that—you know, a friendship bracelet or whatever." She smiled. "Actually, just about the only piece of jewelry I've ever seen her wear— except for that ring her mother left her, I mean, and that African pendant from her great- grandmother—was our old Saddle Club pin." When they were younger, Stevie, Carole, and Lisa had formed a group called The Saddle Club, mostly to give themselves an excuse to talk about horses all the time. The club had never been particularly formal, but the girls had bought matching horse-shaped club pins as a symbol of their friendship. Stevie's pin still held a spot of honor on her bulletin board above her desk.

"Don't be so literal," Alex said with a snort. "I'm not saying you should get her jewelry. I'm just saying you shouldn't limit yourself to all that practical stable stuff. Get her something goofy like a T-shirt with Samson's picture on it or something."

"Samson's picture!" Stevie suddenly hopped off the counter and clapped her hands. "That's it!"

Alex sat up straight in his chair and gave her a surprised look. "Huh?" he said. "I was sort of kidding about the T-shirt. I just meant—"

"I know, I know." Stevie waved her hands to silence him. "But you gave me a great idea. You

127

know how Carole wants to spend all her time with Samson. So why don't I help her with that? I can have Lisa take a really nice photo of him—you saw those awesome pictures she took of Prancer a few months ago. Then I'll have it blown up and framed. Maybe I'll even get one of those two-part frames and put a copy of his pedigree in the other side."

Alex looked impressed. "Hey, that's actually not a bad idea."

"Don't sound so surprised." Stevie grinned at him and tapped herself on the forehead. "I've always been the genius in the family, remember?" She headed toward the phone and grabbed it, planning to call Lisa right away and enlist her help.

"Hold it, genius," Alex said, grabbing the phone out of her hand. "Aren't you forgetting something?"

"Oops." Stevie suddenly remembered that she was grounded. And her parents had given her a dirty look earlier when she'd asked permission to call Phil, which meant there wasn't much point in asking for another exception to the no-phone-calls rule now. "Okay," she said with a sheepish grin. "So maybe I'll talk to Lisa about this tomorrow when I see her at the stable."

She felt a little impatient—after all, Carole's

birthday was less than a week away—but she forced the feeling down. The important thing was that she'd come up with the perfect gift for her friend. Getting started on it could wait one more day.

EIGHT

Thursday morning before chemistry class, when George appeared at her locker as usual, Callie decided it was time to make good on the previous day's vow. "Hi, George," she said, grabbing her lab notebook and slamming her locker shut before turning to face him. "I'm glad you're here. I need to talk to you about something."

"Sure," George said, smiling eagerly. "What is it?"

Callie hesitated. She'd been thinking about this conversation since the night before, but she still wasn't sure what to say. "I'm starting to get kind of worried that maybe you have the wrong idea about our friendship," she said carefully. "It's like I told you. I'm really not interested in you as, you know, a boyfriend or date or anything like that."

A look of intense surprise crossed George's

round face. "I know that," he said. "You explained everything to me last week, remember?"

"Yes, I know." Callie cleared her throat, wishing there were an easier way to deal with these kinds of situations. "But I just wanted to mention it again, just in case. You know, make sure I'd been clear enough."

George raised one eyebrow. "All right, then," he said gently. "If that makes you feel better. But don't worry, you were clear enough the first time. You really don't need to bring it up again."

"Oh. Okay." Feeling desperately awkward, Callie wondered what to say next. "It's just that yesterday, you know, you made such a point of coming over to say hi at the stable. And then there was that phone call the other night. . . ."

George looked astonished. "Is that what this is all about?" he cried. "I already told you—I was just calling because I happened to notice that you hadn't been by the stable for a couple of days. I mean, I know that therapeutic riding you've been doing can't be easy, and I was afraid you might have gotten discouraged." He gave her a bemused smile. "How about this? I promise not to call you again after, say, nine P.M. unless it's a life-or-death emergency. And you promise not to worry too much if my watch is slow and I accidentally call you at nine-oh-one."

Callie felt like the biggest idiot on the planet,

not to mention the world's least grateful friend. Could that be all there was to this after all— friendly concern? Could she really have been mistaken about George's intentions? She supposed it was possible. After all, until moving to Willow Creek she'd never had that many platonic male friends, aside from her brother.

But I do have some pretty good guy friends now, she thought uncertainly. *And Alex Lake doesn't stop by my locker to walk me to class on a daily basis. Phil Marsten isn't always calling just to say hi and see if I'm okay. Even my girlfriends aren't nearly as attentive to my every thought and emotion as George is.*

Still, she reminded herself, she'd always recognized that George was a little different. He had his own way of looking at the world. Why should she expect him to act just like everyone else she knew?

"Okay," she told him. "No biggie. I just wanted to make sure we understood each other."

"Oh, you don't have to worry about that. I understood perfectly." George paused as they reached the doorway of their chemistry classroom and glanced over at her. "Okay, then." He gave a small, polite cough. "Are we cool now?"

"Sure," Callie said. "Of course."

She hurried into the classroom and took her usual place, smiling blandly as George settled himself on a seat beside her and started chattering about the upcoming horse show. *Maybe I am just looking for trouble*, she thought, still feeling a little confused about their whole conversation. *Maybe I just need to relax and accept George for who he is.*

A little later that day, Carole scanned the final essay on her history test. Then she glanced at the classroom clock and smiled. There were only a few minutes left in the period, but for once she had finished with time to spare instead of scribbling desperately until the last possible second. It was a good feeling, especially since she was pretty confident that most of her answers were right.

So this is how Lisa feels all the time, she thought as she set down her pencil and sat back in her chair, rubbing her hands, which were stiff from writing. *No wonder she actually likes school!*

Carole was glad that she'd been prepared for the test, despite the fact that she'd had to cram study sessions in between chores at Pine Hollow, extra practices for the Colesford show, and all her other homework. She was proud of herself when she thought back—especially of the way she'd managed to concentrate on actually *studying* during her study halls that week instead of daydreaming about the horse show or plotting out her Pine Hollow schedule as she usually did.

Thinking about Pine Hollow reminded her of Starlight, which reminded her of her conversation with Tanya Appel the evening before. Tanya had called during dinner, which had caused a few awkward moments.

"Carole's eating dinner right now," Colonel Hanson had said pleasantly after answering the phone. "Can I have her call you back in a little while?" He had listened and then scribbled down the name, looking puzzled. "All right, Tanya. Does she have your number?"

Carole's mind had frozen at the sound of Tanya's name. A moment later, when her father resumed his seat and casually asked who Tanya was, Carole hadn't been able to respond for a moment. After choking out a few unintelligible syllables, she'd finally managed to blurt, "New girl—uh, intermediate class. Pine Hollow."

Her father had raised an eyebrow. "Oh?" he said. "Don't you like her?"

"Uh—what?"

Colonel Hanson shrugged. "You look a little upset," he said. "Isn't this Tanya a good rider?"

"She's fine," Carole had answered quickly, perhaps a little too quickly. Her father had let the topic drop after that, though he'd given her one last curious—or was it suspicious?—glance.

Carole had waited until her father was busy in

his home office that evening before returning Tanya's call. It turned out that Tanya was still just as enthusiastic about Starlight as she'd been earlier. In fact, she wanted to set up an appointment to have her vet look at Starlight the very next evening.

Talk about things moving fast, Carole thought now, staring at her test paper without really seeing it. Instead, she was seeing a vision of Starlight's familiar head with its lopsided star. *I never expected to find a buyer this soon, especially one who's so gung-ho about getting him as soon as possible. It's weird—I feel like I barely know who this Tanya person is, and she might end up being Starlight's new owner.* She shook her head thoughtfully. *I still sort of wish Rachel Hart were a better possibility.*

She guessed that was why she'd put Tanya off, saying she'd call her back today after school and let her know if she could work the vet check in that evening. She hadn't been prepared to face the idea of losing Starlight so soon. After all, if he vetted out okay that evening—and there was no reason to think he wouldn't—Tanya would probably want to close the deal just as quickly. Starlight could be hers by the weekend.

Still, Carole reminded herself, maybe the timing was all for the best. She rested her elbows on her desk and thought about it, trying to put her own emotions aside as much as she could. As much as she wished she could sell Starlight to Rachel, that scenario didn't seem likely to happen anytime soon, if ever. Meanwhile, the Colesford Horse Show was that weekend, and Carole and Samson would probably do well. They might even end up with a ribbon. What better time to spring the news about selling Starlight on her father and Max? And what better time— flushed with victory, just a few days before her birthday—to ask her father to help her buy Samson?

The bell rang at that moment, startling her out of her thoughts. As she passed her test paper forward and gathered her books, Carole still had no idea what she was going to say when she called Tanya a little later that afternoon.

"That lab wasn't as hard as I thought it was going to be," Lisa commented to a classmate named Gary as they walked out of their physics class.

Gary nodded. "Tell me about it," he said. "I may pass this class after all."

Lisa opened her mouth to answer, but just then she caught a glimpse of Carole emerging from a classroom down the crowded school hallway. It was hard to see from this distance, but Lisa thought she looked kind of upset. Suddenly remembering her friend's big history test, Lisa frowned with concern. "Excuse me," she told Gary. "I'll see you tomorrow, okay?"

She hurried toward Carole, catching up to her near the stairwell. Carole looked up and smiled when she saw her. "Hi, Lisa," she said. "How's it going?"

"Okay." That wasn't exactly true—Lisa had had another big fight with her mother that morning at breakfast, and she was still fuming over Alex's sudden change of heart about her college plans, but she figured all that could wait. "What about you? How did your test go? It was today, right?"

"Huh?" Carole blinked, then nodded. "Oh, yeah. Just finished. It was fine—I actually think I did pretty well." She crossed her fingers and held them up with a grin. "I'll find out tomorrow, I guess."

"That's great." Lisa shifted her backpack to her other shoulder and peered into her friend's face. "I'm glad. When I saw you coming out of the room, you looked sort of worried, so I thought . . ."

Carole smiled ruefully. "I am sort of worried, actually," she admitted. "Not about the test, though. I was just thinking about Starlight." She glanced around cautiously, but none of the students rushing by was paying the least bit of attention to their conversation. "That girl Tanya—you know, the one Stevie's cousin told her about? She loved Starlight when she rode him, and she wants her vet to come see him tonight."

"But that's great!" Lisa said, trying to sound as though she meant it. She still had trouble accepting the fact that Carole was really selling Starlight—he'd been around for so long that Lisa had just assumed he would always be at Pine Hollow, just like Prancer or Belle or Barq or Topside or any of the other horses. "The sooner you get it settled, the sooner you can talk to Max about selling you Samson, right?"

"That's what I've been telling myself," Carole agreed, leaning against the wall and hugging her books to her chest. "But I can't help thinking about Rachel Hart. She really loved the idea of buying Starlight. I know he'd be a good match for her." She shrugged. "But who knows how long it could take her to convince her parents to buy her a horse?"

Lisa shook her head. "You don't know," she said. "They may never agree. That's why you shouldn't waste one minute waiting around for her or worrying about what she wants. You have to do what's right for you—forget about anybody else."

Carole looked surprised. "What do you mean?"

Realizing that her words might have sounded a little blunt, Lisa tried to explain. "It's like with me and college. Other people have their needs and opinions and whatever, but I have to forget about that and do what's right for me. Only I can really know what that is."

She thought back to some of the comments her mother had made that morning. Mrs. Atwood still seemed to think that Lisa had made some sort of careless, seat-of-the-pants decision, one that was destined to ruin her life. Lisa didn't know how to get through to her—to convince her that she was the one who would have to spend four years at the college she picked, and nobody else could understand all the things that would mean to her. That was why she'd made this decision alone and why she was standing up for it now. After all, if she didn't, who would?

Suddenly, though, Lisa remembered that there was one more viewpoint Carole had to consider in her own situation. "Unless you think this buyer is wrong from Starlight's perspective," she added. "You know, if he seemed to dislike her or something like that, or if she was mean to him."

"No, that's not the problem. He seemed to like her fine." Carole bit her lip and gazed down at her books. "I mean, I don't have strong feelings about Tanya one way or the other. I hardly know her. But I know Rachel, and I know she could learn a lot from a horse like Starlight. And I know she'd treat him right."

"All right, then. If this Tanya girl is a serious buyer and you're serious about selling, then that should be that." Lisa snapped her fingers to emphasize her point. "Other people are always going to have other needs and opinions and everything, but you can't let that stop you from getting what *you* want."

Carole still seemed surprised at Lisa's declaration, and perhaps a bit puzzled as well. "But I'm not sure this is the same sort of . . . I mean, no offense, and I see your point and everything, but I can't help thinking it all sounds kind of, you know, selfish or something."

"Only if you think it's selfish to stand up for yourself," Lisa replied firmly. "Look at it this way. The big horse show is this Saturday. You're going to ride to win, right?"

Carole shrugged. "Of course."

"Right. Of course. Why else would you bother to enter?" Lisa said. "You probably won't spend one second worrying about hurting your competitors' feelings or whatever because that would just mess you up in the ring—make you lose, compromise your own performance." She smiled grimly. "So that's what you've got to do with this Starlight thing, too. Take care of yourself first and don't worry about what everybody else thinks. That's the only way to win."

NINE

"Hi, Tanya?" Carole said, gripping the receiver and glancing cautiously toward the office door. She had closed it behind her when she'd entered, but that didn't mean much. Denise or Red or Max himself could burst through it at any moment looking for some paperwork or needing to use the phone.

"Carole!" Tanya sounded thrilled to hear from her. "What's up? Did you check your schedule? I talked to my vet, and she can come by just about anytime you want, but I told her I was hoping we could do it tonight. So what do you say? Are you free or what? Because I really want to move on this right away."

Carole waited until Tanya paused for breath, then jumped in. "Tonight's fine," she said quickly. "Why don't you bring your vet by around seven o'clock? Is that okay with you?" She figured that by then most of the people at Pine Hollow would have left for the day. Max would be up at the house tucking his daughters into bed, and Red and Denise would probably be busy with the evening feeding. With any luck, nobody would even notice Tanya and her vet.

"Sure!" Tanya sounded thrilled. "That would be perfect. I just hope I can stand the suspense between now and then! But I'm sure Starlight will vet out just fine. I have a really good feeling about it."

"I don't think you have to worry," Carole agreed. "Starlight's the healthiest horse in the barn. But it's best to get a vet's opinion before you buy. My dad did the same thing before he bought Starlight for me."

"Okay," Tanya said brightly. "Well, I'll see you and Starlight tonight. I can't wait!"

"Right. See you then. Bye."

Carole put down the phone and stared at it for a second. Then she rubbed her eyes, feeling a sudden wave of sadness wash over her. She already knew that Starlight was perfectly sound— there was no way Tanya's vet was going to find anything wrong with him. That meant there was really nothing standing in the way of the sale. Her horse could be leaving Pine Hollow soon. For good. Carole had been preparing herself for just that event for a while now, but she still couldn't quite believe it was really going to happen.

When she looked up again, Carole almost jumped out of her chair. Ben was standing in the office doorway, his expression hovering between uncertainty and embarrassment.

"Sorry," he said gruffly at her gasp of surprise. "Didn't mean to scare you. I didn't know—uh, anyway. Sorry."

"That's okay." Carole put a hand on her heart, which was beating fast. "Um, you just startled me, that's all. I didn't hear the door open."

"Not just that," Ben mumbled, his voice so low she could hardly make out his words. "Sorry about, you know. Starlight. It must be tough. Now that it's really happening. I'm—I hope you're okay."

Carole realized that he must have overheard at least part of her conversation with Tanya. She flashed back to Lisa's comments earlier that day. At first she had thought her friend's advice seemed too hard-hearted. But maybe she had a point. "I'm fine," she told Ben, doing her best to sound normal and upbeat. "It's all for the best. I mean, I'm getting what I wanted. And that's good, right?"

"Sure." Ben looked a little surprised. "But still, you know—well, you know. I just wanted to say something. In case you want to talk or—or anything."

"Thanks, but I'm fine," Carole said briskly, pushing back the office chair and standing up. "Well, I'd better stop sitting around and get to work. I have a ton to do today."

"Whatever." Ben shrugged and turned away quickly.

As he did, Carole caught a flash of an odd expression on his face. Was it confusion? she wondered. She thought it was, at least partly. But she also couldn't help thinking he looked a little bit hurt as well.

Oops, she thought, feeling bad. She hurried to the office door. *I guess he really wanted to help. Maybe I shouldn't have been so quick to blow off his sympathy. It's not like he offers it all that often.*

But it was too late now. Ben was already disappearing around the corner at the end of the hall. Carole bit her lip, realizing she'd been so wrapped up in her own problems that she hadn't even noticed how nice was Ben was being—or at least trying to be—until she'd scared him off.

Then her mind flashed back to the image of Tanya soaring over those jumps the day before on Starlight, and she suddenly felt tears well up in her eyes. She could worry about Ben later. Right now she had more important things to deal with. Like figuring out how she was going to be able to say good-bye to her horse.

———

Lisa pressed her foot down on the brake, bringing her car to a halt behind a pickup truck that had stopped at a red light. As she idled, waiting for the light to turn green, her mind wandered back, once again, to her argument with her mother that morning.

You're not thinking straight, Lisa, Mrs. Atwood had said through clenched teeth. *You're going to regret this someday. I just want to save you from that. I know how these things work. So why won't you listen to me?*

Because you don't know how these things work, Lisa had replied hotly. *You don't know what it's like to be me. You don't have my life. You may think you know what I need, but you don't. Only I know that.*

Mrs. Atwood had smiled bitterly at that. *You're the one who thinks only you know what's going on here*, she had told Lisa. *You think you have your whole life all figured out. You think you're making all the right moves. But all you're doing is closing off your options. And for what? A high-school romance. You're letting someone else control your life.*

"If she only knew," Lisa muttered, clutching the steering wheel more tightly. After all, Alex didn't even seem to want her to go to NVU anymore. That didn't mean she was changing her mind, of course. It didn't change anything.

The light flashed to green, and Lisa followed the truck into the intersection, taking the familiar turn toward home. She glanced at the packet of freshly developed photos on the seat beside her; she'd just picked them up at the drugstore. Before that she'd bought herself some new school notebooks at the stationery store and dropped off her good white blouse at the dry cleaner's. She only wished she had more errands to use as an excuse for not going home.

Then again, why do I need an excuse? she asked herself, blinking at the road in front of her. *I'm almost an adult, right? If I don't feel like going home and waiting for Mom to get home from work so that she can start yelling at me again, maybe I should just go do something else for a while.*

But what? She was tempted to stop by Pine Hollow and visit Prancer. But she realized she didn't particularly feel like running into either of her best friends at the moment. She was sure that Alex must have told Stevie by now about their little scene the previous afternoon. Besides that, she was starting to wonder if maybe Carole and Stevie might have some doubts about her college plans, too. They had seemed glad and supportive enough when she'd first told them of her decision, but they hadn't said much to her about it since. That wasn't really like them. And hadn't there been something a little odd about the way

147

Carole had looked at her earlier when she'd mentioned her plans?

Stop being paranoid, Lisa told herself, squeezing the steering wheel. *You're just looking for trouble.* Still, she passed by the road to Pine Hollow without so much as a glance.

A few minutes later she reached the turnoff for her own street, but instead of making the turn, she kept going straight, planning to loop around the long way instead. That would kill a few more minutes.

Once it had occurred to her, she couldn't quite shake the thought that her best friends weren't acting quite the way she might have expected them to when it came to her college plans. In fact, nobody was reacting to her news the way she'd thought they would—not Alex, not her parents, not her friends. She'd thought her decision would make them all happy. Instead, they all seemed to think she'd royally screwed up her life.

But they're wrong, she told herself. *Aren't they?*

At that moment a bird flew across the road right in front of her car, low and fast. Lisa automatically tapped the brakes, even though the bird was already across. As she moved her foot back to the gas pedal, she glanced in the direction the bird had gone and noticed a sign indicating the way to Highway 12. The quiet two-lane country road ran past the Willow Creek Mall and then continued northwest as far as New Salisbury, the town where NVU was.

As she read the sign, something suddenly clicked in Lisa's head. "What a great idea," she said aloud. "I'll drive up to NVU for the afternoon."

As soon as she said it, she felt better. It was the perfect way to kill two birds with one stone. She could postpone the next round with her mother while also reminding herself of what she'd actually chosen, instead of focusing only on what everybody else claimed she was giving up.

At the next stop sign, Lisa leaned over and flipped open the glove compartment, feeling around inside until she located her cellular phone. Her father had bought it for her the day she'd gotten her driver's license, ordering her to keep it in the car at all times in case of emergency. Lisa often forgot it was there, though she'd learned to appreciate it late one stormy night the previous spring when her tire had blown along a deserted stretch of highway between her house and the mall. She had been able to call for help instead of struggling to change the tire on her own.

Now she dialed her home number and waited for the answering machine to click on. "Don't be there. Don't be there," she muttered, hoping

149

that her mother hadn't decided to take another day off from work.

After four rings, the machine clicked on. Lisa left a brief message after the beep, telling her mother that she would be at Pine Hollow for the next several hours helping her friends get ready for the horse show, and that she might not be home for dinner.

I just hope Carole or Stevie won't call before I get home, she thought as she turned off the phone and slid it back into the glove compartment. *If they do, Mom will probably freak out and think I got into some horrible accident on my way to the stable. Either that or she'll figure out that it was all a cover story.*

Still, she couldn't manage to worry about that too much. In fact, she thought it might do her mother good to get a taste of how a typical teenager operated. Then maybe she would appreciate that Lisa really was pretty mature and responsible most of the time—the kind of girl who was more than capable of making important decisions all by herself.

Gunning the engine as she shot across the intersection and headed for the access road leading to the highway, Lisa did her best to forget about the present and the past and think only of the future. She had been to NVU a number of times before, but she was sure she would see it in a whole new light now that she knew she'd be spending the next four years of her life there.

It only took her an hour to reach the edge of the NVU campus. She quickly found a parking spot in the visitors' lot near the football stadium. Climbing out of the car, she stretched and glanced around, slipping on her jacket against the slight autumn chill. Then she locked her car, dropped her keys in her purse, and headed across the parking lot, following a sign pointing the way to the Center Green.

The campus was bustling. Most classes were over for the day, and students were everywhere—walking back to their dorms, rushing to the library or an early dinner at the dining hall, or just hanging out on the grass with friends, enjoying the pleasant evening. Lisa moved among them, strolling down the wide brick-paved walkway that meandered in and out and around the broad, tree-studded swath of lawn known as Center Green. Buildings of every conceivable vintage ringed the green, from the ivy-twined stone walls of the venerable eighteenth-century edifice that housed the admissions offices and other administrative departments to a modern glass-and-steel structure that, if Lisa recalled correctly from her campus tour the previous spring, was the new home of the university's law school. Somehow all the disparate architectural styles worked together, creating a vibrant, interesting picture.

Lisa traveled the full circle around the green, checking out each of the buildings she passed. She remembered most of them from her tour and other visits—the library, the student life building, the science center. She also kept a wary eye on the students all around her, not really wanting to run into anyone she knew. Still, she wasn't particularly worried. The population of NVU was large enough that she knew her chances of accidentally encountering Chad Lake or any other acquaintance were pretty slim.

Once she'd completed her walk around Center Green, she headed down an offshoot of the walk that led between the English department building and the student health office toward East Campus, where most of the freshman dorms were clustered around a parklike area surrounding the main dining hall.

I wonder which of these dorms I'll live in next year? Lisa thought, wandering off the path and pausing on a slope near a small, picturesque pond. More than two dozen students were sprawled on the grass on the pond's banks. Several of them were reading or studying. A couple of small groups were chatting with each other. One solitary guy was wearing headphones, tapping his foot as he bit into an apple. Another guy was sound asleep on his back, completely oblivious to the couple making out passionately nearby.

After looking around at the dorms for a few minutes, wondering what it would be like to live in one of them, Lisa turned her gaze to the low, concrete bulk of the dining hall across the grass. As the hour grew later, more and more students were hurrying through the building's wide glass doors. Lisa's stomach grumbled, and she realized she was getting hungry.

Too bad I'm not a student here yet, she thought ruefully, rubbing her stomach. *I don't care how much Chad complains about college food. I could really go for a nice dining hall burger or something right about now.*

Fortunately, she knew she had other options. The town of New Salisbury, like most college towns, contained plenty of casual restaurants and fast-food places that catered primarily to cash-strapped students, so Lisa was sure she could grab a quick and inexpensive dinner before heading back to the parking lot for the drive home to Willow Creek. In fact, she remembered that once last year, when she had driven up with Stevie and Alex to visit Chad, he had taken them out to a terrific burger-and-pizza place near his dorm. That meant it had to be somewhere nearby. But where? Lisa turned slowly in a circle,

153

frowning slightly with concentration as she tried to remember in which direction they had gone.

"Hi there." An unfamiliar voice interrupted her thoughts. "I don't usually walk up to strange girls like this, but I couldn't help noticing that you looked a little lost and thought you could use some help." Lisa turned to see a tall, broad-shouldered guy in a rugby shirt smiling at her. He gave her a winning smile. "My name's Rick, by the way."

"I'm Lisa," she offered, smiling back tentatively. "And I'm more hungry than lost. I was just looking around for someplace to grab a quick burger or something."

"Well, then you're in luck, Lisa." Rick's smile broadened. "Because I happen to be on my way to just such a place. In fact, they may serve up the best burgers in the county. Want to join me?"

Lisa gulped nervously. "Um, I'd better not," she said, not wanting the friendly student to get the wrong idea. "Thanks anyway, though."

"Are you sure?" Rick shrugged and ran a hand over his straight, sandy brown hair. "I'm just meeting my girlfriend and a couple of my housemates there—no big deal. They won't mind if you tag along."

Girlfriend? Lisa relaxed immediately, feeling slightly foolish for jumping to the conclusion that the guy was hitting on her just because he was being nice to her. "Well, if you're sure they won't mind," she said slowly. The thought of going to a real college hangout with real college students made her feel mature and slightly daring. She liked the feeling. "That would be really nice."

"Cool. Come on, it's this way." Rick loped off, and Lisa had to break into a trot to keep up with him.

He led her straight past the dining hall and a cluster of dorms to the edge of campus. After crossing the street, they walked another block or two until they reached an area packed with small shops, restaurants, and bars.

"Here we go." Rick gestured to a tall, narrow building with a neon sign reading Old Dominion hanging over a green-painted door. "This place gets pretty crowded at night, but we're early, so we should get a seat." He pushed open the door and held it for Lisa to walk through ahead of him.

As far as Lisa could see, the restaurant consisted of one long, narrow room. A large, ornately carved bar ran the length of the left side, with bar stools lined up all along it. At this early hour, only a few people were perched on the stools, with beers or paper plates full of french fries in front of them. The other wall was lined by a row of deep vinyl-upholstered booths with glass-shaded overhead lamps hanging over each scarred wooden table. Several of the booths were occupied by groups of laughing, talking people, mostly students. The warm smell of frying beef mixed with the slightly sour odor of stale beer and tickled Lisa's nose, making her stomach growl more than ever.

"Cool place," Lisa commented, raising her voice slightly to make herself heard above the din.

Rick smiled. "Just wait until you taste the food." He gestured for her to follow him toward a booth halfway down the wall. Three other students were already seated there—a pretty, olive-skinned girl with cat's-eye glasses, and two good-looking guys, one with broad shoulders and close-cropped blond hair and the other African American with shoulder-length dreadlocks and serious brown eyes.

"Yo, guys," Rick greeted them. "This is Lisa. I kidnapped her from the green and forced her to come eat with us."

The girl—Lisa assumed she was the girlfriend Rick had mentioned—looked up and smiled. "Hi, Lisa. I'm Safiya. You'll have to excuse Rick—he loves picking up strays, even when they don't actually need rescuing. I hope you didn't have other dinner plans he dragged you away from."

Lisa smiled, feeling a little intimidated by the other girl's exotic good looks but reassured by her warm words and sincere smile. "No, I didn't have plans," she said. "Actually, I'm just here visiting by myself." She had explained her visit to Rick on the walk over, and he quickly filled in his friends. Then he introduced the two guys, whose names were Teddy and Paul.

"So you're a senior in high school?" the big blond guy, Teddy, asked as Lisa took a seat beside him in the booth. "Where do you go?"

"Willow Creek High," Lisa said, accepting the menu Safiya handed her across the table. "It's about forty miles from here."

Teddy shrugged and smiled, revealing a pair of perfectly matched dimples in his beefy cheeks. "Never heard of it."

"I have, I think," Safiya said. "A girl on my freshman hall last year went there. Do you know Melissa Overbrook?"

Lisa nodded, vaguely recalling a rowdy, athletic girl who had been two years ahead of her in school. "I know who she is," she said. "But I didn't really know her."

"What about Kevin Hart?" the other guy, Paul, asked. "He's in my English seminar."

Lisa smiled in surprise. "Of course!" she said.

"I mean, he actually didn't go to my school, but he's from Willow Creek—the town, I mean. His little sister rides at the same stable as I do."

"You ride?" Safiya looked interested. "Sweet. That must be so amazing. Do you have your own horse?"

For the next few minutes, Lisa fell into a comfortable discussion of the familiar subjects of horses and riding. From there, the conversation wandered naturally to other topics. The college students were happy to answer all the questions Lisa could come up with about NVU, and the more she talked to them, the more excited she felt about starting college. In fact, she was beginning to wish she could enroll right then and there—hanging out with her new friends on campus definitely sounded better than going back to Willow Creek and dealing with all the annoying and unpleasant problems awaiting her there.

Still, she did her best to forget about her meddling mother, her unsupportive boyfriend, and the high-risk pregnancy of her horse-to-be for the moment and just enjoy herself. It wasn't that hard once she got started. She really liked Rick, Teddy, Paul, and especially Safiya. The older girl was so friendly and smart and funny that Lisa was already starting to think of her as a friend.

"How did you end up choosing NVU?" Lisa

asked after Safiya finished a hilarious story about her first day at college, when she had dragged three overstuffed suitcases into the engineering building, thinking it was her dorm. "I mean, what made you decide to go here instead of somewhere else?"

Safiya shrugged and took a sip of her iced tea. "It was pretty easy, really," she said. "I want to be a nurse, but I also wanted to go to a regular four-year school—you know, have the whole college experience. NVU has a really good undergraduate nursing program. Just about the only places better are Penn and Michigan, and they both turned me down."

"Oh." Lisa felt a little bit awkward about having brought up the subject when she heard that. Still, Safiya didn't seem upset or embarrassed about it, so Lisa figured she didn't mind. "Well, I'm glad you're here now, anyway."

Safiya smiled at her across the table. "Me too."

"Me three," Rick added, leaning over to plant a kiss on Safiya's cheek. "If you'd ended up at Penn or Michigan, we never would have met."

Paul rolled his eyes. "And the romance of the century would never have occurred," he said dryly as he grabbed a handful of fries off Rick's plate.

Safiya ignored him. "We still would have met,

sweetie," she said, grabbing Rick's face and turning it toward her to plant a big kiss on his lips. "We would have found each other somehow. Fate, you know."

Lisa smiled as she watched them. She thought she knew exactly what Safiya meant. It was the same way she felt about Alex. Even if he hadn't been her best friend's brother, even if he hadn't lived just a few doors down from her, she couldn't quite believe that they wouldn't have ended up meeting and falling in love anyway. She knew it even when she was really annoyed with him, the way she was at the moment. . . .

As she continued to chat with her new friends between bites of her delicious burger, Lisa automatically scanned the restaurant once again, looking for familiar faces. Now that she was here and having such a good time, she thought she might not mind running into Chad or one of her other acquaintances. The only person she really wanted to avoid, of course, was Rafe. But she was pretty sure he was working that night, so she wasn't too worried.

But this time she did spy someone else she knew—someone she wasn't expecting to see there. "A.J.?" she muttered with a slight frown, hardly believing her eyes.

But it was definitely Phil's friend A.J. who had just walked into the place with a couple of other guys. There was no mistaking his reddish brown hair and thin, energetic form. As Lisa watched, A.J. and his companions slid onto some stools at the bar and said something to the bartender. The bartender cocked his head at A.J. and one of the other guys, looking skeptical. But when A.J. and his friend flashed their IDs, the bartender shrugged and walked over to the tap. Before long he had filled three mugs and set them in front of the trio.

Lisa's mind reeled. She was surprised to see A.J. there at all, so far from home, but what was he doing drinking beer? He was sixteen, a year younger than she was. Besides, she would have thought he'd learned his lesson at the Lakes' party, when he'd drunk too much beer and ended up being escorted home by the police. She watched out of the corner of her eye as A.J. and the other two guys sat there and drank their beers, then ordered a second round.

"Lisa?" Rick said, poking her on the shoulder. "What's wrong? Looking for an escape route? Don't go—I promise I won't let Teddy start talking about his econ midterm again. That could scare anyone away."

Lisa forced a smile. "It's not that," she told her new friends. "Um, I see someone I know over there at the bar. Excuse me a minute. I think I'll go say hi."

She slid out of the booth and made her way toward A.J., wondering what to say to him. She hadn't seen him since the party, but she knew he'd been unpredictable ever since finding out that he was adopted. Sometimes he seemed almost like his old, friendly, funny self, while at other times he was a virtual stranger, sullen and bitter. Still, she couldn't just ignore the fact that he was there. She had to try to talk to him.

There was an empty stool next to him, and she stopped beside it. She cleared her throat. "Hi, A.J.," she said.

A look of surprise and dismay flickered across his face when he saw who had greeted him, but then he shrugged and smiled. "Yo, Lisa," he said. "What are you doing here?"

"I was just about to ask you the same thing." Lisa did her best to keep her tone casual.

A.J.'s two companions had leaned over curiously to see her. Lisa noted that one of them was a guy she'd seen around town at parties and other events. A.J. jerked his thumb at the guy. "You've met Jeremy Castle, right? He's a senior at Cross County. Jer, Lisa Atwood. And that's his older brother Caleb. He goes to school here."

"Hey there, Lisa," Jeremy said, smiling and blinking and leaning closer, almost shoving A.J. off his bar stool in the process. "Why don't you join us? You can sit right here with me." He patted his lap invitingly.

"No, thank you." Lisa did her best not to shudder. The way Jeremy was looking at her made her feel like one of the burgers on the restaurant's menu. Ignoring both Jeremy and his older brother, who was gazing at her curiously, Lisa focused on A.J. "Look," she said in a low voice, "I don't know what's going on, but I really think you ought to get out of here. I'll give you a ride home if you want."

A.J. shook his head and lifted his beer. "No thanks," he said. "I've still got work to do here."

"But you're—" Lisa shot a quick glance at the bartender, making sure he was out of earshot. The last thing she wanted to do was to get A.J. busted again. He had enough problems as it was. She lowered her voice still more. "How did you get served, anyway?"

A.J. grinned, took a swig from his mug, and then set it down. He reached into his pocket and pulled out a card. "Check it out," he said, handing it to Lisa.

She took it and saw that it was a driver's license with A.J.'s picture on it. But instead of being from Virginia, it was from Oregon. And instead of A.J.'s real name and age, the card listed him as Michael O'Reilly, age twenty-two.

"Are you crazy?" Lisa whispered, handing it

163

back to him quickly. Even holding it made her feel nervous and somehow dirty. "That's a fake ID!"

"Isn't it cool?" A.J. returned the card to his pocket, still grinning. "Caleb got them for us. Ten bucks. Great deal, huh?"

Just then Caleb leaned forward. "Ready for another round, dude?" he asked A.J. "I'm buying."

"Sure," A.J. said, quickly draining the rest of the beer from his mug and wiping the foam from his mouth with the back of his hand. "Hit me with it."

"What about you?"

With a jolt, Lisa realized that Caleb was addressing her. "What?" she asked, startled.

Caleb spoke very slowly, as if talking to a slow two-year-old. "Do—you—want—a—beer?"

"No," Lisa replied quickly. "No thanks. And A.J. isn't having any more either."

"Huh?" A.J. frowned at her. "Who are you, my mother?"

"Yeah, Mama!" Jeremy hooted, pounding his hand on the bar and almost upsetting his beer mug. "Hey, Ma, will you change my diapers?" The other two guys started laughing; then Caleb turned away to signal the bartender.

Lisa gritted her teeth. "A.J.," she said as calmly as she could, "I really don't think you

164

want to do this. Why don't you come with me? My car's just across campus. We can talk about this on the way back home."

"Is that a threat?" A.J. said, smirking. "Because I think I'll pass. I'm not in the mood for a chat right now."

"Are you crazy, dude?" Jeremy shoved A.J. in the side. "She just invited you back to her car!" He leered at Lisa. "Forget about him. I'll come home with you, honey."

Lisa sighed, forcing herself not to snap back a sharp retort. It wasn't worth it. Jeremy was either already drunk or just a jerk. Either way, he wasn't her problem. But she was really worried about A.J. As obnoxious as he'd been acting lately, he was still her friend.

Still, there didn't seem to be anything she could do for him right then short of turning him in to the campus police. "How are you getting home?" she asked him.

A.J. shrugged. "Don't know. I'm probably not," he said. "Caleb said we could crash at his place tonight. He lives off campus." He seemed very impressed by that fact.

Just then the bartender slid another beer in front of him. Lisa shot the man a desperate look, wishing she could just blurt out the truth—that A.J. and his friend were underage, that their IDs were fake. But she couldn't bring herself to do it.

She turned away, comforting herself with the idea that at least A.J. and Jeremy wouldn't be trying to drive anywhere that night. Of course, that meant they were probably planning to skip school the next day, but that was the least of Lisa's worries.

"Okay," she told A.J. "Well, I can't force you to come with me. So I'll see you, okay?"

As she walked away, she thought she heard Jeremy make some comment about how she could force him anytime, and then a snort of laughter from A.J. But she didn't look back.

When she returned to the booth, Lisa realized she wasn't in the mood to play coed anymore. Suddenly her fun, grown-up college adventure didn't seem that exciting, and all she wanted to do was get home, call Stevie, and tell her about A.J. She only hoped Stevie's parents would let her talk. After making a quick excuse to her new friends and exchanging phone numbers with Safiya, Lisa hurried out of the restaurant and headed for her car, hardly noticing the softly glowing campus lights blinking on all around her as dusk fell.

TEN
10

Carole glanced out the office window over Max's shoulder. A light but steady drizzle had been falling all afternoon, and the heavy cloud cover made it look a lot later than it actually was. That wasn't helping anyone's mood at Pine Hollow—the show was the next day, and there was still so much to do that it was making everyone a little frantic.

And as if I don't have enough to worry about already, just getting myself and Samson ready, Carole thought, twisting her hands together nervously in her lap, *I just can't stop thinking about that vet check last night.*

She forced herself to tune back into Max's speech. She didn't want to miss anything important because she was obsessing over Tanya's visit. ". . . and I just want you all to remember," Max was saying somberly, tapping a pen slowly against his desk for emphasis. "Competing at a show of this importance, against riders of this caliber, is going to be a great challenge. But you shouldn't think of it as a contest against others. I really want you to focus on bettering your*selves*, concentrating on improving your own . . ."

Carole's mind drifted again. She had heard Max give the same speech, or some version of it, more times than she could remember. She couldn't seem to concentrate on his words this time, not when her mind wouldn't stop worrying over the fact that Starlight would soon belong to someone else.

The vet check had gone perfectly smoothly, just as Carole had anticipated. Once the doctor had pronounced the gelding sound and healthy, Tanya had practically gone ballistic with excitement. She'd been ready to pack Starlight into her mother's car right then and there—or at least return to pick him up as soon as possible. Part of Carole wanted to go along with that plan, thinking it might be easier to do it fast, like ripping off a bandage all at once. But she couldn't quite bear the thought of losing Starlight amidst all the preshow commotion. So she had insisted that Tanya wait to pick him up until Saturday evening, after the show was over and Carole could give her horse a proper farewell. She hoped that would also give her enough time to break the news to her father and Max. Somehow, she couldn't quite picture how Max would react if a van arrived to pick up one of his boarders without his knowledge.

Tanya had clearly been unhappy with the delay. But she had reluctantly agreed on the condition that she could bring her father by Pine Hollow on Friday afternoon to show him the horse he was buying her. Carole hadn't been able to argue against that, so she had set up the visit for a little later that afternoon.

Heaving herself up a little straighter in her chair, Carole glanced around the room at the others. Stevie was sitting in the chair beside her, fidgeting and looking slightly impatient. George was standing quietly against the wall of bookshelves, both hands in his pockets and a serene expression on his round face. Denise was perched on a stool she'd dragged in from the tack room, picking at her fingernails but otherwise seeming more attentive to Max's words than the others. Ben, as usual, looked impassive and unreadable as he leaned against the door frame.

Carole sighed as Max started talking about goals and challenges. Sneaking a peek at her watch, she could only hope that he would wind things up soon so that she would have time to finish some chores before Tanya arrived.

While Carole was watching the clock, Stevie was thinking about her plans for her friend's birthday gift. She had made some progress in the last two days, but she knew she still had more to do if she wanted to be ready in time. On her way home from Pine Hollow the day before, she had made a quick detour to the nearby shopping center and bought a nice frame. She had also managed to sneak Samson's folder out of the stable office and make a quick copy of his entire pedigree on Deborah's copier up at the house, pretending she was doing some kind of school project.

It had been a lucky break to stumble upon a note in the shirt pocket of her thirteen-year-old brother, Michael, while she was doing laundry on Wednesday evening. That was how she had discovered that Michael's girlfriend, Fawn, was really talented with a calligraphy set. Michael had been irate that Stevie had been snooping in his private correspondence, but Stevie had ignored him and gone directly to Fawn, who lived across the street. Fawn had gladly agreed to copy out Samson's pedigree in fancy script, and Stevie had to admit that the younger girl had done a fantastic job. The pedigree looked professional and gorgeous, and she was sure that Carole would love it.

Now the only missing piece of the puzzle was the photo. Stevie's parents had banished her and Alex to the pool shed for most of Thursday afternoon, ordering them not to return to the house until the messy building was organized and spotless, so Stevie hadn't even been able to get near the phone, let alone call Lisa. She knew that she was running out of time—during her trip to the shopping center, she'd discovered that the photo shop within the local drugstore was closed on Sundays, and that it took at least twenty-four hours to have a print blown up to the size Stevie wanted. That meant she needed to get the film over there by Saturday at the latest, and that day was going to be pretty well occupied by the horse show.

That means I've got to get the film to the developer today, she thought anxiously, playing with the ends of her dark blond hair as Max droned on and on about the true meaning of success. *I don't have time to track Lisa down.* Instead, Stevie had decided to take the picture of Samson herself. Her father's camera was tucked into her backpack right now, sitting in her cubby in Pine Hollow's locker room. All she had to do was find a free moment to use it.

Glancing at the window behind Max, Stevie saw that the sun had finally peeked out from behind the clouds. It was the perfect moment to capture Samson on film. She had seen him in the back paddock, where Carole must have turned him out earlier to stretch his legs. Although her fingers itched to grab the camera and rush out there, she forced herself to stay put and pretend to listen. She would find the right moment just as soon as Max let them go. If he ever let them go . . .

At that same moment, Callie was in the indoor ring with Maxi. The two of them were mounted once again on Windsor and Krona, practicing basic riding skills. Callie still couldn't get over how quickly the little girl learned. She also couldn't quite get over how much she herself was enjoying playing teacher. In fact, she'd had such a good time earlier that week that she had volunteered to watch Maxi today while Deborah worked on her article, and again the next day at the horse show.

It will be fun to watch the show through her eyes, Callie thought, gazing across the ring at Maxi, who was carefully posting to Krona's quick, slightly choppy trot. *I'm sure she's going to love every second of it. She can't stop talking about how excited she is that we're going together. I really think she thinks of me as her new best friend.*

She smiled at the thought. But her smile faded a bit as she remembered another friend who would be at the show the next day. George's behavior hadn't changed much since Thursday morning. He had still showed up that morning to walk her to chemistry class, and he saved her a seat beside him at lunch. If he'd been offended by her accusations the other day, he certainly wasn't showing it, and Callie was grateful for that. She still couldn't believe the way Scott had gotten her all worked up about George's intentions.

Just because Scott scams on practically every girl he meets, he shouldn't assume all guys are the same way, she thought with a flash of irritation, not even caring that she was exaggerating at least a little bit. *Thanks to him, I ended up looking totally paranoid. I'm just lucky George is nice enough to pretend it never happened.*

Despite her thoughts, however, Callie couldn't help a slight, nagging feeling that something about her friendship with George still seemed odd. But she did her best to ignore that twinge of hesitation, telling herself it was just a lingering result of her little talk with her brother.

Poor George, Callie thought, blinking at Maxi as she posted by, but not really seeing the little girl. *All he wants is to be my friend, and I can't stop being suspicious of him.*

She decided it was time to change that. Maybe she would never really be able to appreciate George as much as he deserved, but she was going to do her best. She could start by being extra nice to him at the horse show tomorrow. Maybe that would make up for how weird and wary and indecisive she'd been acting toward him lately.

Stevie thought Max would never stop babbling on about self-improvement and good sportsmanship, but finally he released them from the meeting. After a hurried good-bye to the others, she raced out of the office and down the hall. She quickly grabbed her father's camera out of her cubby, then made her way across the entryway toward the aisle leading to the back entrance. This time she forced herself to walk at a leisurely pace, not wanting to rouse any suspicions about what she was doing.

"Stevie!" Max called to her from the hallway near the office.

Stevie stopped short halfway across the entryway, feeling guilty. She was sure that Max would be less than thrilled if he found out she was spending time snapping photos when she should be getting herself and Belle ready for the show. Hiding the camera behind her back, she turned and smiled innocently at him. "Hi, Max," she said. "Great speech back there. Very inspirational."

"Thanks," Max said dryly, making Stevie wonder if he'd noticed that she had spaced out through most of his talk. "Look, if you see Carole before I do, could you ask her to bring Prancer in from the west paddock?"

"Sure thing!" Stevie agreed brightly. As soon as Max turned away, she continued on her way.

As soon as she took the turn into the stable aisle, she spotted Carole. Stevie quickly hid the camera behind her back again, though this time she needn't have bothered. Carole's complete attention was focused on the horse she had just put in cross-ties, a young dapple-gray mare named Firefly. The temperamental mare obviously wasn't in the mood to be groomed at the moment, and she was letting Carole know it in no uncertain terms.

"Are you okay?" Stevie asked with concern as Firefly shifted her hindquarters, almost stepping on Carole's foot. Carole jumped out of the way just in time, but the grooming bucket wasn't so lucky. Firefly's hoof grazed it, tipping it and spilling its contents onto the ground.

Carole glanced up and saw Stevie watching her. "Hi," she said through clenched teeth as she kicked a stray currycomb out of the path and then moved to Firefly's head, where she began stroking the mare's neck soothingly. "We'll be fine. Firefly's really feeling her oats today, that's all, and she's still not crazy about this whole grooming deal. But she'll settle down soon—she always does."

"Okay." Stevie started to duck past them, then paused. "Oh, by the way," she said, "Max was looking for you. He wants you to bring Prancer in from her paddock."

"He does?" Carole glanced from Stevie to Firefly and back again, looking desperate. "Yikes. I hate to ask, but would you mind getting Prancer? It's going to take me a while to finish here, and then I promised Denise I'd help her give Talisman a bath—you know how he hates water. And Tanya's coming by in a little while. . . ."

"Enough said," Stevie said quickly, sensing that her friend was on the verge of losing it. Things were always pretty crazy around the stable right before a show, and Stevie couldn't even imagine the added pressure that was on Carole as she went through the painful process of selling her horse at the same time. "I'll get her."

"Thanks," Carole said gratefully before turning her attention back to Firefly.

Stevie glanced at her watch and then hurried on her way. She was going to have to work fast. The photo shop closed in less than an hour.

Luckily she didn't pass anyone else on her way to the back paddock except for a couple of intermediate riders. Samson was standing in the middle of the small enclosure, dozing in the weak sunbeams struggling to break through the cloud cover.

"Say cheese," Stevie muttered, raising the camera and snapping a couple of shots of the muscular black horse at rest.

Then she called to Samson to wake him up, hoping to get a few slightly more active poses. Samson obliged by trotting toward her to say hello, then stretching his legs by circling the ring before settling down to graze. Stevie used up the entire roll of film, getting a few close-ups and a lot of full body shots. When she heard the camera click into rewind mode, she nodded with satisfaction.

"That should do the trick," she muttered to herself. She might not be the photographer Lisa was, but it wasn't as though her gift required some kind of fancy artistic composition or anything. Carole would be thrilled just to have a good, clear photo of her favorite horse to hang on her wall, and Stevie was sure she would be able to find a nice image out of the ones she'd just taken.

It seemed to take forever for the film to rewind. Finally the camera clicked off, and Stevie opened the case and removed the roll, tucking it into her pocket for safety.

Glancing at her watch, she saw that time was short. Alex had the car that day—her parents had wanted him to run errands for them after school again—so Stevie was going to have to walk, or rather run, over to the shopping center to drop off the film. It wasn't a long way, but closing time was approaching rapidly.

"Feet, don't fail me now," Stevie murmured as she headed around the side of the stable building toward the driveway. Partway there, she happened to glance out at the fields and paddocks ranged around the building. Several horses were grazing there, and suddenly Stevie remembered her promise to Carole. "Prancer!" she whispered, smacking herself on the head.

She wasn't sure what to do. The photo shop would close soon. Did she have time to walk out to the west paddock, round up Prancer, and settle her in her stall? She didn't think so. *Maybe I should go to the photo shop first and then come back and get Prancer*, she thought, anxiously checking her watch again. *Of course, that will make me late getting home, and it's my turn to cook. . . .*

Her thoughts were interrupted by the sounds of giggling from nearby. Wandering forward, Stevie saw that a couple of intermediate riders, Juliet Phillips and Alexandra Foster, were standing near the parking area, drinking sodas.

Getting a sudden flash of inspiration, Stevie

raced over to them. "What are you guys doing right now?" she demanded.

Juliet looked startled. "Nothing, Stevie," she said. "Honest. We were just talking."

"Yeah," Alexandra said. "Juliet's mom is coming to pick us up in a little while, and, well . . ." She traded a sheepish glance with her friend. "Actually, we're waiting out here because, you know . . ."

"You didn't want to get stuck doing stable chores." Stevie almost smiled. Cleaning tack and mucking out stalls weren't anybody's idea of a good time, especially late on Friday afternoon. But she forced herself to look disapproving. "Hmmm. You know what Max would say about that. We're all supposed to help out around here. It's what keeps Pine Hollow running."

"We know," Juliet said. She gazed at Stevie beseechingly. "You aren't going to turn us in to Max, are you?"

"Not if you do me a favor," Stevie replied briskly. She jerked her head in the direction of the west paddock. "Go get Prancer and put her away in her stall. How about it?"

"Sure." Alexandra looked relieved. "We can do that."

"Good." Stevie was relieved, too. As the younger girls turned and made their way toward the paddock, Stevie spun on her heel and jogged down the driveway. Now she would definitely be able to make it to the photo shop on time.

Carole headed down the aisle toward the wash stall. She still had a few minutes before she was supposed to meet Denise for Talisman's bath, but she figured it wouldn't hurt to start warming up the water now. Talisman was one of Pine Hollow's most reliable, talented, and experienced competition horses. But like many horses, the athletic chestnut gelding had his quirks, which in his case included an intense distaste for baths. Actually, he wasn't crazy about water in any incarnation, although Denise had worked with him to the point where he would tolerate putting his foot in a stream or a water jump. But he was always the first horse under shelter whenever it started to rain, and the stable staff was under strict orders that nobody should try to bathe him on their own.

Carole knew he needed a bath that day if he was going to look his best when Denise rode him in the show. She was always glad to help, although just this once she couldn't stop herself from wishing that Denise had asked someone else. There was so much to do, and then there was Tanya's upcoming visit to worry about on top of it all.

As Carole passed Starlight's stall on her way to

the wash stall, she stopped short in shock. Tanya was already there, running a rag over the gelding's back and making his already spotless mahogany coat gleam. A man in an expensive-looking business suit was leaning on the half door, watching.

For a second, Carole felt a sharp flash of annoyance. Couldn't Tanya wait even one more day before she started acting like Starlight was her horse?

Then the anger passed as quickly as it had come. *Of course she can't wait another day*, she thought. *Neither could I, if I were in her place. And I wouldn't want it to be any different. It shows how excited she is to have him, and how crazy she is about him. Those are good things.*

Glancing at her watch, which showed that Tanya was more than half an hour early again, Carole bit back a sigh and then stepped forward to introduce herself to Mr. Appel. As she chatted politely with Tanya's father, Carole caught a glimpse of Max hurrying by at the end of the aisle. She also saw him do a double-take when he spotted the strange man standing in his stable aisle. But he didn't do more than shoot Carole a curious glance before hurrying on, and Carole was glad. She was lucky that Max was too busy to come over and see what was going on, or her secret would have been out.

"Hi, Carole." Tanya grinned, letting herself out of the stall and stuffing her grooming rag into her jeans pocket. "Sorry I'm early again. I just couldn't wait to see Starlight again."

Carole forced a smile. "That's okay," she said. "So, are we all set for tomorrow evening?"

Tanya nodded. "Daddy arranged to borrow a horse trailer from my riding instructor. Right, Daddy?"

"That's right, pumpkin." Mr. Appel smiled indulgently at his daughter.

Tanya grabbed her father's arm and squeezed it fondly before returning her attention to Carole. "And there's a stall all ready for him at my stable," she said. "All I have to do is get a nameplate."

"Don't bother." Carole's voice sounded a little weak, even to herself, as she imagined Tanya leading Starlight into a strange stall at a strange stable. She gestured at the brass nameplate on the wall nearby. "You can have this one. I'll make sure someone unscrews it for you by tomorrow night."

"Really?" Tanya's eyes lit up. She reached out and ran her fingers over Starlight's name, which was etched in the brass. "Thanks, Carole! That's so nice. And don't worry—if you miss Starlight when he's gone, you can come visit him anytime." Before Carole could answer, Tanya clapped her hands and laughed out loud. "I'm so excited!" she cried, grabbing Carole by the arm. "This is so amazing. I can't believe I'm really getting my own horse. Isn't it cool, Daddy?"

Mr. Appel nodded. "Of course, pumpkin," he said. "I just hope you're sure this is the horse you really want." He cast an uncertain glance at Starlight.

Tanya ignored him. "Let's make it official, okay?" she told Carole. She giggled. "Whenever Daddy makes a business deal, he seals it with a handshake. Right, Daddy?"

"That's right, pumpkin." Mr. Appel looked amused. "You two go ahead and shake, and then we'd better get going. We'll talk about your new horse more later."

"Okay." Tanya stuck out her hand. "Deal?"

Carole stared at it for a long second. This was it. With this handshake, she would know that the deal was final. Starlight wouldn't be hers any longer. He would belong to Tanya, for better or for worse.

Then she remembered the other side of the equation. When Starlight belonged to Tanya, that would mean Carole would be free to go about making sure that Samson would soon belong to her. She grasped Tanya's outstretched hand in her own and pumped it firmly. "Deal."

Soon after that, with a flurry of good-byes, the

Appels left the stable. Carole slumped against the wall outside Starlight's stall, feeling deflated and empty and a little sick. She had done it. Starlight was really going. Even though she'd been preparing herself for this feeling ever since she'd made the decision to sell her horse, she still couldn't believe how much it hurt. She couldn't even bring herself to glance into Starlight's stall, to see his familiar quizzical expression and big liquid eyes, the lopsided white star splashed across his face. She rubbed her eyes hard, willing herself not to break down and cry. This wasn't the time or the place for that. Keeping her fingers pressed against her eyelids, she took several deep, gulping breaths, trying to settle her stomach and her heart.

"Carole?"

For one crazy moment, Carole had the wild idea that it was Starlight himself who was calling her name in that low, tentative voice. Her eyes flew open, and she saw Ben standing in front of her, looking worried.

"Oh!" she exclaimed, feeling a blush steal over her cheeks. "Um, I was just—that is, I—"

"I know." Ben took a step closer. "I saw her leave. Are you okay?"

Carole looked up at him, surprised to find that instead of having its usual guarded expression, Ben's face was open and worried. She stared into his dark eyes, wondering what he would say if she told him the truth. That she wasn't okay—she felt sad and confused and guilty and even, strangely, a little angry, and she wasn't sure how to handle it. It would be nice to talk to someone who might understand what she was feeling. And for some reason, as he held her gaze with his own, she thought that Ben might understand. More than that, she realized that she *wanted* him to understand.

"Well," she began hesitantly, still not sure what she was going to say. "I—"

"Carole!" a gleeful young voice interrupted from the end of the aisle. Carole glanced away from Ben, startled. A moment later Maxi raced up and flung herself at Carole, wrapping her arms around her waist. "Guess what? Callie taught me how to make Krona lift up his foot." Behind the little girl, Carole could see Callie hurrying down the aisle.

For a split second, Carole caught Ben's eye again. But she could see that it was already too late. The moment had passed. The curtain was down again, and his expression was closed and remote.

ELEVEN

After a week of mostly cloudy, drizzly weather, Saturday morning dawned miraculously sunny, clear, and cool. Carole arrived at Pine Hollow early, and so had the other four competitors. Max and Red were there, too, already looking harried.

Carole got right to work on Samson's grooming, but she had trouble concentrating on the task. Her mind kept wandering to the strange, restless dreams she'd had the previous night. A few had been typical preshow jitters playing themselves out, but most of the dreams had involved Tanya and Starlight and sometimes Samson. Carole couldn't remember many of the details, but the dreams had left her feeling unsettled and vaguely apprehensive.

I've got to focus, Carole thought, blinking at the big black horse in front of her as he shifted his feet, obviously bored with standing still while she worked on his mane. She patted him and

186

spoke to him soothingly, and he settled down, though she could tell that he was still feeling a little impatient. He was real, and this was no dream. She had a show to get ready for, and she wasn't going to get everything done if she wasted time worrying about some stupid dreams.

Deciding that the best way to snap out of it was to think about something practical, she turned her mind to the clothes and equipment she would need for today's show. She knew that Samson's tack and equipment were all ready and packed—she'd checked and double-checked it the day before, and checked it again first thing that morning. Besides, she knew herself well enough to realize that if she was going to forget something, it was more likely to be something for herself than for her horse. As she continued to work steadily on Samson's mane, she ran down the list out loud. "Good breeches. Good boots. Shirt, jacket, gloves . . ."

By the time she finished her list and was confident that she'd remembered everything she was going to need, thoughts of the dreams were starting to recede. Carole didn't have time to think about them anymore. There was too much to do.

Somehow, everybody got everything done. Carole emerged from the bathroom, where she'd splashed most of the dirt and sweat from her face, just in time to hear Max and Red pulling two of Pine Hollow's horse trailers around to the front of the stable. Hurrying outside, Carole found Stevie watching, hopping excitedly from one foot to the other.

"It's almost time!" Stevie said cheerfully when she spotted Carole. "Ready to go show those snooty show-circuit folks what Pine Hollow can do?"

Carole nodded, trying to remember if she'd packed extra hairbands in case the one she was wearing broke. "I think so."

"Don't just *think* so!" Stevie playfully poked Carole in the chest. "Know so!"

Carole grinned. So far that morning she'd only seen Stevie a few times in passing. But now she could tell that her friend was in an excited, giddy mood. And who could blame her? "Okay," Carole said with a professional-looking military salute. "I *know* so. *Sir!*"

Max hopped out of the Pine Hollow station wagon, which was pulling one of the trailers, and spotted them. "Where are the others?" he called.

"I think they're all still inside," Carole replied. She'd seen Denise in the bathroom brushing her teeth. George was in the tack room. And as far as she knew, Ben was still in Topside's stall, whispering to the bay gelding in a language only horses could understand.

Max glanced at his watch. "We'd better start loading soon," he said. "I'm taking this trailer, and Denise can drive the other one." He nodded toward Red as the head stable hand climbed out of Denise's truck, which was hitched to the second trailer. "Red's going to stay here to take care of morning chores and look after the other horses until the other hands get here. He'll join us at the show grounds a little later."

Carole just nodded. Out of the corner of her eye, she thought she caught Stevie rolling her eyes. Max had gone over all this several times yesterday, and again first thing this morning. Still, Carole didn't blame him. Better safe than sorry. "I'll go tell Ben to bring Topside out," she offered. "You want to load him first, right?" At Max's nod, she turned to hurry back into the building.

The next few minutes were taken up with loading the horses. Topside was the most experienced show horse in the group, and a calm and reliable loader, so Ben had no trouble leading him up the ramp into Max's trailer. Next, Denise brought out Talisman. The lanky chestnut was younger and more excitable than Topside, but he entered the trailer willingly enough, standing quietly in the stall beside the older gelding. George's Trakehner mare, Joyride, was known to be difficult to load, and it took a few minutes to coax her up the ramp and get her settled. But George was patient with her, and with the others standing by to help, the tricky task was accomplished without too much trouble.

"Okay," Max said as he helped Ben swing the trailer door shut. "We're going to get going. Will you be okay loading Belle and Starlight?"

"Samson," Carole corrected quickly.

Max smiled. "Sorry. I'm so used to you and Starlight traveling as a pair. Well, you know. Anyway, Red and Denise can help you."

"We'll be fine." Stevie shooed him toward the station wagon. "Go already."

As soon as Max drove down the driveway, with Ben in the car beside him, Stevie and Carole went inside to get their horses. As Carole led Samson out of his stall, she could see that the black gelding was alert and feeling frisky. "That's right, big guy," she whispered as they moved down the stable aisle. "It's the day we've been waiting for."

She felt a thrill of anticipation run down her spine, making her shiver. All those hours of practicing and training were about to pay off. When she and Samson stepped into the ring, she knew they would be ready to give it their best shot.

Soon the horses were safely settled in the trailer, and Carole and Stevie were crowded into the long front seat of Denise's truck. "Ready to hit the road?" Denise asked as she turned the key in the ignition.

"Let's roll," Stevie said gleefully. She let out a whoop as the truck's engine roared to life. "Yee-hah!" she cried.

Carole laughed, her spirits rising as her friend's excitement rubbed off on her. She couldn't totally forget what she had to do later, after the show was over. But she also knew there would be time to feel sad about losing Starlight then. Right now, she wanted to savor every moment of her first big show with Samson.

I can't wait, she thought as the truck rumbled down the driveway. *Even if we don't win a thing, I'm sure this show is going to be one of the greatest experiences of my entire life!*

"I think it's cute that you've finally discovered your maternal instincts, sis," Scott said, spinning the steering wheel to take the turn into Pine Hollow's driveway. "It's about time."

Callie rolled her eyes. Scott had been teasing her all morning about her baby-sitting duties. But she didn't really care. She was looking forward to spending time with Maxi during the horse show. "You're just jealous because nobody wants to hang out with you at the show," she

191

informed him. "You're lucky Maxi and I are letting you tag along."

Scott grinned good-naturedly as he brought the car to a stop in the parking area. As he unhooked his seat belt, he glanced toward the main stable building. "There's your tiny admirer now," he said.

Callie looked over as she gathered her crutches. Maxi was sitting on the wooden bench outside the stable's main entrance, her legs swinging an inch or two above the hard-packed ground. Callie opened the car door and called to the little girl.

"Callie!" Maxi cried, hopping down from the bench and rushing toward the car. "I thought you'd never get here."

"We're here now," Scott said cheerfully. "Now all we have to do is grab Lisa and we can go. Is she here yet, Maxi?"

Maxi nodded. "She's with Red. They're looking at Prancer."

Callie checked her watch. "We're a little early," she told Scott. "Let's give her a minute." Lisa had called the evening before to suggest that they all ride over to Colesford together to watch the show. Normally, Callie was sure that Alex would be part of the group, too. But because of his grounding, he was riding over to the show with his parents and younger brother.

Callie and Scott spent the next few minutes chatting with Maxi and enjoying the breezy but sunny autumn morning. But after their meeting time came and went and there was still no sign of Lisa, Callie offered to go inside and find her.

Leaving Maxi chattering to Scott about all the horse shows she and Krona were going to enter someday, Callie swung toward the entrance. As she often did lately, she tested herself by putting most of her weight on her right leg before setting down the tip of the crutch. *No doubt about it,* she thought with satisfaction. *I'm not going to need these stupid things much longer. I told Dr. Amandsen I'd be walking on my own way before January!*

Pushing those thoughts out of her mind for the moment, she pushed open the stable door and hurried across the entryway toward the aisle where Prancer's stall was located. As she rounded the corner, she spotted Red O'Malley coming toward her.

"Hi!" Callie called, a little surprised that he hadn't left for the show with the others. He and Denise had been a couple for years, and Callie was sure that Red would want to watch her performance. "What are you still doing here?"

Red blinked and looked up, seeming a bit startled by her greeting. "Oh! Hey there, Callie," he said. "I'm supposed to head over to Colesford soon. Just have to take care of a few things first."

Callie knew that Red had been working for Max longer than any of the other staff, and he often stepped in when Max was busy or away. At the moment she couldn't help thinking that the responsibility was weighing on him heavily—he looked tired and worried. "Have you seen Lisa?" Callie asked him. "Maxi said she was in here. She's riding over to the show with us."

"Actually, there's been a slight change of plans," Red said, rubbing his face with one freckled hand. "Prancer's running a fever, so Lisa's going to stick around until Judy gets here. I'll give her a ride to the show when I come."

"Oh. Okay." Callie felt a twinge of concern for the pregnant mare. Still, she was sure that Judy Barker would know what to do for her. And she didn't blame Lisa for wanting to stay and wait for the vet. It was obvious how much she cared for Prancer. In her place, Callie would have done the same thing. "Well, I guess we'll see you both later, then," she told Red, already turning to head back outside. "And tell Lisa I hope Prancer feels better soon."

The first class wasn't scheduled to start for some time, but the show grounds just outside the town of Colesford were already bustling

194

when the Pine Hollow trailers arrived. Carole's heart hammered in her chest as she looked out the truck's windows and tried to see everything at once. They had entered via a narrow dirt drive, passing a sign reading Competitors Only. Soon they'd come through a small stand of thick forest into view of the huge, open area of the show grounds. In the distance, Carole spotted the tall bleachers that surrounded the main competition ring. She had only been to the show grounds once before, when a traveling circus had set up there, but she imagined that the rows of wooden booths outside the main ring were probably bustling with vendors selling programs, food, and souvenirs. At the moment, though, Carole was a lot more interested in the area just beyond their truck. Several good-sized practice rings were laid out in a wide, flat field. Countless horse trailers and vans were lined up in the park-like stable area on the near side of the practice rings, while across the way Carole saw a line of long, low wooden stable buildings that she assumed were to house the competitors who'd come from far enough away to have to stay overnight. Everywhere Carole looked, horses and people and dogs were moving around, stretching their legs and getting ready for the big show.

"Wow," Stevie said, neatly summing up the entire scene. "I can't believe we're really here."

"Believe it, ladies," Denise announced, carefully steering over a rutted stretch of the dirt road and peering out at the numbers flapping from the trees they were passing. "Because it's true. Now help me find our section."

Carole pointed, spotting an open space to their left. "There," she called. "I see the other trailer just ahead. See?" She waved at George Wheeler, who had just spotted them and was waving both arms over his head to signal to them.

Denise braked just enough to allow a frisky corgi to race, barking, across her path. Then she drove toward George, who stepped back to let the truck pull into the spot beside Max's car.

"We thought you'd never get here!" George exclaimed as Stevie rolled down the window to greet him.

"Hey, they wouldn't start the show without us," Stevie said breezily, leaning out the window to look around. "Where are Max and Ben?"

"Ben's walking Talisman to settle him down," George said. "I don't know about Max. After we got the horses unloaded, he saw someone he knew and took off."

Carole was hardly listening. She poked impatiently at Stevie until she finally climbed out of the truck, and then Carole hopped out after her. Hurrying around to the back of the trailer, she swung open the door and stepped inside. Samson and Belle were standing quietly, only their pricked ears revealing their curiosity about what was going on around them. Carole smiled as she looked at Samson. Even in the dimness of the van, she could tell that he was alert and spirited. He was just as ready for today as she was.

A little while later, all the Pine Hollow horses were settled in their temporary quarters. Max was still nowhere to be found, so Carole and Stevie decided to take a quick look around before it was time to warm up and get changed.

They strolled down the row of vans and trailers, checking out the competition. Carole recognized a number of horses and riders from shows she'd attended in the area, and a few from seeing them on TV and in equestrian magazines. She and Stevie wandered all the way to the edge of the wooden buildings, where many stables had hung signs or flags outside their blocks of stalls.

Carole scanned each stable name as they walked. "It's hard to believe we're going to be riding with people from places like Five Springs Farm—that's Garrett Shanahan's stable's name." She pointed to the sign they were passing at that moment. "He's that awesome show jumper from Canada," she told Stevie. She shook her head in disbelief. Garrett Shanahan had been on the circuit for years, and he had always been one of

Carole's heroes. "I mean, just think of it. Me, riding the same course as the famous Garrett Shanahan!"

Stevie shook her head and grinned. "That's not what's hard to believe," she said. "What's *really* hard to believe is that my parents have given me a whole day of freedom from my grounding. I don't even have to think about chores until tomorrow."

"Except stable chores," Carole corrected with a grin. But she was still thinking about Garrett Shanahan. She glanced around, hoping for a glimpse of her idol. But the only person in view was a wizened old stable hand. "I wonder what horse Garrett will be riding in Open Jumping?" she commented. "That real famous jumper of his—you know, Cloverleaf, the big bay with the funny spot on his forehead—just retired. At least that's what I read."

Stevie shrugged. "I guess you'll find out soon enough." She grinned. "Why? Getting nervous?"

"No way," Carole replied automatically. And she realized it was true, at least in part. She was always a little bit nervous before any show, of course. That was normal. But the thought of competing against well-known, talented, experienced riders like Garrett Shanahan didn't scare her nearly as much as she might have expected.

I know exactly why that is, too, she thought as

she wandered down the dusty path after Stevie. *It's because I'll be riding Samson. I may not have as much experience as some of the others, but that doesn't matter, because I know that my horse*—she paused in the thought for a moment, smiling to herself at how natural it felt to use the possessive when she was thinking about Samson—*Well, he's almost mine, anyway. And I know he can do just about anything!*

TWELVE

Lisa was as scared and worried as she'd ever been in her life. "Is she going to be okay? What do you think is wrong?" she asked Red for about the sixth time. "She was fine last week."

Red shook his head grimly. "Who knows?" he said. "We all know this pregnancy is risky. And we've had scares before. I suppose it could be nothing again, like those times." He rubbed his ear and stared at the mare. "But this fever can't mean anything good."

Lisa swallowed hard and returned her gaze to Prancer. The mare was obviously in distress. Her body glistened with a light coating of sweat, and her head drooped. *How did this happen?* Lisa thought. *I haven't seen her up close for a few days, but other people have. This must have happened suddenly—literally overnight. But why? What's wrong?*

She didn't know the answers to those questions, and it was clear that Red didn't, either. "I wish Judy would get here," Lisa said softly, stretching her hand over the stall door to pat Prancer. The mare's flank shuddered at her touch, and Prancer took an awkward step away from the door, out of reach.

Red shot Lisa a sympathetic look. "Try not to worry," he said, though Lisa thought he looked awfully worried himself. "Judy will be here soon. She was over at the racetrack when I got through on her portable phone, but when I told her what was going on, she said she was leaving right away."

As if on cue, Judy Barker's voice rang out from the direction of the entryway. "Red?" she called, sounding breathless. "Where are you?"

"Down here!" Red called, loud enough to cause Prancer's ears to flop uneasily toward him. "We're with Prancer."

A moment later Judy appeared, dressed in jeans and a flannel shirt and carrying her black medical bag. "Hi," she greeted Red briskly. "Oh, hi, Lisa. I didn't know you were here, too. I thought everyone had already left for that show."

Lisa just shook her head wordlessly. In her worry, she had almost forgotten about the horse show. When she had arrived at Pine Hollow that morning, half an hour before she was supposed to meet Callie and Scott, she had been excited about watching her friends compete and having the chance to spend some time with Alex, even though she still felt a little weird about his reaction to her college plans.

But all that had flown out of her mind as soon as she'd reached Prancer's stall and found Red there, looking anxious. He had made his morning rounds soon after Max and the others had departed, and that was when he'd noticed that Prancer had barely touched her breakfast. That alone was cause for worry, but the mare's haggard appearance had prompted him to get in touch with the vet immediately, especially when he determined that Prancer was running a fever.

As Judy opened the stall door and walked toward Prancer, crooning to the mare soothingly, Lisa crossed her fingers and tried not to panic. All she could hope was that she and Red were all worked up for nothing—that the vet would quickly diagnose something minor and innocuous and put their fears to rest.

"Wow." Judy let out a low whistle as she ran her hands over the mare's neck and sides, looking her over. "How long has she looked like this?"

Red shrugged. "She seemed okay yesterday," he said. "I mean, it's been a little crazy around here this week. But she's been eating, and nobody has noticed anything odd."

Judy nodded, looking grim. "I haven't seen

her in almost a week myself," she commented tensely. "I wish . . ." Her voice trailed off, and she turned to glance at Lisa. "Could you hand me my bag please?" she asked. "I want to see if I can figure out what's going on here."

Lisa hoisted the black bag, which was sitting in the aisle. It was surprisingly heavy, but she hardly noticed as she passed it over the half door. All she could think about was Prancer.

At that same moment, Carole and Stevie were making their way back to the Pine Hollow trailers. Carole checked her watch and saw that they still had plenty of time before they needed to start getting ready for their first events. "Hey, why don't we go check out the refreshments?" she suggested, suddenly remembering that she'd only had time to gulp down half a banana that morning before leaving for the stable. "We don't need to get down to work for half an hour at least."

"Sounds like a plan," Stevie agreed. "Let's check with Denise and the others and see if they want us to bring anything back."

"Okay." Carole glanced down at her watch once more, just to make sure her time calculations were right. When she looked up again, her eyes widened as she took in their home base. She had just seen that Max had returned from wherever he'd gone earlier—and he wasn't alone.

"Check it out!" she whispered, grabbing Stevie by the arm.

"Ow!" Stevie protested, yanking her arm away. "What are you trying to do, cripple me right before my big Colesford debut?" She rubbed her arm, looking disgruntled.

Carole didn't pay any attention to her friend's complaint. She was still staring at Max and his companion—a tall, distinguished-looking man with wavy brown hair and a flawless tweed riding coat and cuffed jodhpurs. "Do you know who Max is talking to?" she whispered excitedly. "It's him. Garrett Shanahan!"

Now Stevie looked interested. "Really? Wow. I didn't know Max knew him."

Carole shrugged. She hadn't known that, either, but she wasn't particularly surprised. Max had once competed at the highest levels himself, and several well-known riders had gotten their starts at Pine Hollow, including the retired show jumper Dorothy DeSoto. Maybe Dorothy had introduced the two men at some show or other.

As Carole and Stevie came closer, Denise spotted them and hurried over. "Did you see?" she murmured, casting a glance over at Max.

"I know." Carole grinned. "Mysterious Max strikes again. Who knew he had so many famous friends?" It was tempting to hang around and wait for a chance to meet the famous Garrett Shanahan, but Carole's stomach grumbled, and she knew she'd better get some food into it before things really got started. "Hey, is everything under control around here?" she asked Denise. "Stevie and I were just going to walk over and grab a snack."

"Everything's fine," Denise assured her. "The horses have all settled down nicely, and Ben had the station wagon unpacked before we even got here. Go ahead."

"Can we bring you anything?" Stevie asked.

After Denise placed her order for bottled water and onion rings, the girls moved on. They found George, who asked them to pick him up some potato chips. Finally they came to Ben, who was sitting on a stool in the shade of the trailers, polishing his boots.

"Hi," Carole said, realizing she'd barely spoken to Ben since that weird moment the day before. "Um, we're making a food run. Do you want anything?"

Ben glanced up briefly. "No," he replied, his voice gruff. Then he returned his gaze to his work without another word.

Stevie rolled your eyes. "You're welcome," she muttered under her breath.

Carole's face flamed, and she shot a glance at

Ben, hoping he hadn't heard. She couldn't tell—
his expression hadn't changed a bit, but that
didn't mean much. Grabbing Stevie's arm, Carole dragged her away.

"Should we ask Max if he wants anything?"
Carole asked, glancing again at the stable owner.
He still seemed to be deep in conversation with
Garrett Shanahan.

Stevie shrugged. "Let's just bring him a soda,"
she suggested.

Carole agreed, and the two of them set off
once again down the long row of trailers. This
time they walked straight past the stable buildings and through the gate leading to the public
area of the show grounds. They were both wearing the tags Max had passed out identifying
them as competitors, which meant they would
have no trouble getting back past the gate again.

The show grounds were starting to fill up with
spectators, and the whole place had a carnival
atmosphere. Children and dogs ran around noisily, playing in the grassy areas around the wide
pathways behind the bleachers. Concession
stands lined the paved paths leading from the
main entrance, selling food, programs, T-shirts,
hats, riding gear, balloons, and all sorts of other
souvenirs and trinkets. Carole hardly knew
where to look first.

"This is amazing," she said. "All these people are here to watch us! Us and the horses, I mean."

Stevie nodded. "Let's get a program."

Carole agreed eagerly. Max had posted a schedule listing the times and locations of their own classes, but it didn't say anything about the day's other events. Carole knew that the first competition of the show was scheduled to start in less than half an hour, even though the first Pine Hollow rider wasn't due in the ring until almost noon.

The girls bought a program and pored over it eagerly, planning which events they wanted to try to watch in between their own preparations. Carole smiled when a little girl passed them and squealed, spotting their tags.

"Mommy, look!" the girl said in a loud stage whisper. "Those girls are going to be in the show!"

"Ah, the life of a public idol," Stevie murmured to Carole, making her laugh.

"Speaking of public figures, I think I see a certain politician's son and daughter right now." Carole pointed to Scott and Callie, who each had one of Maxi Regnery's hands. All three of them were smiling and heading toward them, dodging through the crowds.

"Hi!" Scott called. "Hey, shouldn't you two

be off polishing your hard hats or something for your big debut?"

Stevie was glancing past the Foresters, obviously looking for someone else. "Where's Lisa? You didn't forget her, did you?"

Callie laughed. "Of course not," she said. "She should be here soon—she decided to ride over with Red. There was some kind of problem with—"

"Whoa!" Carole exclaimed, interrupting Callie. "I can't believe this. That's my history teacher over there by the pizza stand!"

Stevie shrugged. "So what? A bunch of my teachers said they might come, too. This horse show is, like, the social event of the county."

"No, no." Carole stared at Ms. Shepard, who was about thirty yards away and completely unaware of her presence. "It's not that she's here. It's who she's here *with*." She pointed to the stout, balding man who had his arm tucked protectively around the history teacher's waist. "That's Mr. Whiteside, my algebra teacher! I had no idea the two of them were dating!"

Stevie, Callie, and Scott shot the couple a curious glance, but Maxi clearly had no interest in inter-teacher romance. She tugged insistently on Callie's hand. "Come on!" she cried. "You said we could go see the ponies."

"Okay," Callie told the little girl. She

shrugged apologetically at Carole and Stevie. "Sorry, no time to chat. We've got big plans, as you can see."

Carole grinned. She had already noticed the signs pointing the way to the area where young visitors could go for pony rides. Knowing Maxi, she would want to spend most of the day—and probably most of Callie's and Scott's spare cash—over there. "All right. Just don't get so caught up with those ponies that you forget to watch our classes."

"We won't," Scott promised as Maxi started to drag him and Callie away. "We'll be right there in the stands, cheering you on."

Stevie hardly seemed to notice their departure. She was standing on her tiptoes, glancing around.

"What are you doing?" Carole asked.

"Phil said he'd look for me every half hour by the lemonade stand," Stevie explained. "The only trouble is, it looks like there are two lemonade stands. One right across the path there, and another one way over—"

"Guess who!" Phil cried, appearing suddenly behind Stevie and clapping his hands over her eyes.

Stevie spun around and threw her arms around him, planting a big kiss on his lips. "It's about time you turned up!" she said when she came up for air.

Carole smiled. She knew that Stevie hadn't been able to spend much time with her boyfriend since being grounded. She figured this was a good time to give them a little privacy. "I'm going to see if I can find Dad," she told the happy couple. "He was supposed to ride over with some friends from the neighborhood. I'll pick up the snacks for the others and see you back at the trailers, okay?"

"Uh-huh," Stevie said distractedly, her arms still wrapped around Phil's neck.

Carole moved off, glancing again at her teachers, who were standing under the shade of an awning, munching on gooey slices of pizza. They still hadn't spotted her, and Carole ducked behind the program booth, preferring to keep it that way.

She'd only gone a few steps when she saw her father. He was talking to a couple of friends, but when he saw Carole coming toward him, he left them and came to meet her with a big smile on his face. "How's my favorite champion-to-be daughter?" he asked.

"Great. Isn't this cool?" Carole waved an arm to indicate the noisy, exciting scene surrounding them. "It seems like everybody in the world is here." She grinned. "Even my two lovebird teachers."

"What?"

Carole crooked a finger at her father, gesturing for him to come over to where he could peek around the side of the program booth. "Look over there," she said. "See that woman with the brown hair and blue shirt? That's Ms. Shepard, my history teacher. And the guy she's with is my math teacher, Mr. Whiteside. I didn't even know they knew each other!" She smiled fondly at the teachers, especially Ms. Shepard. She was feeling especially warm toward her because she had handed back that week's history test the day before, and Carole had received an A. It almost made her forget about that other test all those weeks ago.

"Ah." Colonel Hanson smiled and ruffled Carole's dark curls. "Well, I guess that just goes to show that anything can happen at a horse show, huh?"

Carole knew he was just goofing around, but she nodded. "Definitely," she agreed whole-heartedly. "And that reminds me. I've got to get going, or I know one thing that will certainly be happening soon—namely, Max chewing me out for being late!"

Saying good-bye to her father, she hurried

toward the nearest food tent to pick up the snacks before heading back to the stable area.

Lisa willed herself to remain calm as she watched Judy snap her bag shut. She thought she would burst if the vet didn't tell them something soon. Judy had hardly said a word since beginning her examination.

As she left the stall, the vet's face looked pinched and grave. Lisa wasn't sure she dared ask for the diagnosis. Fortunately, Red spoke up. "Well?" he asked quietly. "How is she?"

"I won't lie to you. Things don't look very good, I'm afraid." The vet spoke slowly, forming each word carefully and deliberately. "From what I can determine, it seems that one of the foals has died inside of Prancer, probably over the past couple of days. Since we didn't notice and take action right away, she's gone septic. The infection appears to have spread quickly."

Lisa's mind reeled. "But you can stop it, right?" she asked. "You can give her some medicine or something and stop the infection. Make her better."

Judy heaved a deep breath. "I'll do what I can, of course," she told Lisa somberly. "Prancer has always been strong and healthy. It's possible she'll pull through."

"And the other foal?" Red asked.

Judy shook her head. "There's no telling," she said grimly. "As I said, things don't look very good right now. But at the moment the second foal is still alive."

Lisa hated the pessimistic tone in Judy's voice, hated the thought that Prancer might lose both her foals after coming so far. As for Prancer herself . . . Lisa didn't dare think too hard about that. Prancer had to pull through. That was all there was to it.

Lisa entered the stall and walked up to Prancer, who stood listlessly, her head drooping. As she stroked the mare's head, trying to comfort her as best she could, she was vaguely aware that Red and Judy were talking in the aisle, discussing whether to try to reach Max at the show grounds. But Lisa wasn't paying much attention to them. All she could focus on was Prancer. She had known all along that this pregnancy could be dangerous for the mare. But until now, she had faced that fact only in her nightmares.

Now she was afraid that her worst nightmares might be coming true.

THIRTEEN

From the moment she and Samson stepped into the ring for their first round, Carole knew she'd been right to expect this to be a day she would always remember. When she'd warmed up Samson a little earlier, she had instantly sensed that he was at his very best that day. And Carole was convinced that Samson's very best was just about invincible.

Just as important, Carole felt confident that she had a handle on the course, which was challenging but not unreasonable. Before the event, she had walked it with the other competitors, doing her best not to let herself get distracted by all the famous faces around her. She knew she would have plenty of time to ask for autographs later if she wanted to. For the moment, though, they all had a job to do—herself as much as Garrett Shanahan or any of the others.

Now all the weeks and months of preparation were about to pay off. At the sound of the starting horn, Samson leaped forward eagerly, responding instantly to Carole's signals. He sailed easily over the first fence, a simple post-and-rail. The next few obstacles didn't pose any more of a problem for the big black horse, and Carole felt her optimism soar higher with each jump.

We can do this! she thought, recognizing deep in her heart that it was true. *Samson and I can do this. We really can!*

She yanked her thoughts back to the task at hand. They *could* do it, but it was going to take all her concentration. This was no time to get distracted. The most difficult section of the course was still to come.

Carole tightened up slightly on the reins and quickly estimated their approach to the next post-and-rail. Then she glanced ahead, knowing she would have to be alert for the upcoming triple jump—the angle leading into it was tricky, and many of the riders before her had brought down at least one section.

She cleared her mind of that until Samson had landed safely and cleanly on the far side of the post-and-rail. Then she steadied him, slowing his fast pace slightly and focusing on the strides leading up to the first section of the triple. They had to land perfectly in order to make the single stride between the first and second section work, and Carole was ready. She measured Samson's canter, then signaled for him to extend it slightly.

It worked. The big black horse was controlled and well-positioned as he cleared the first section. After one clean stride, he soared up and over the second section, his hooves not even scraping the top rail. The third section flashed by beneath them just as easily.

After that, even the high puissance wall that came next didn't look the least bit scary. Carole felt more and more confident with each jump, but she was careful not to get overconfident and sloppy. She kept checking and rechecking their position and Samson's stride, making adjustments where necessary. She also made sure to keep Samson moving along as fast as she felt they could go without sacrificing accuracy. The last thing she wanted was to ride clear of jumping faults and lose out by coming in half a second over the allotted time.

Finally, all that stood between them and a clean round—one of the very few so far—was a simple brush fence. It wasn't as high or forbidding as many of the obstacles they'd already jumped, but despite that, it had been the downfall of two or three riders before them. Carole tried not to get nervous as Samson headed toward it, his ears pricked forward. "Steady, big guy," she whispered, even though she knew there was no way the horse could hear her over the pounding of his own hooves. She tried not to think about how disappointing it would be to come this far and then knock down a rail: That kind of thinking would only guarantee a fault.

In what seemed the blink of an eye, there were just four strides left to the fence, then three. Carole forced her nervousness away. She had to do this. She had to do it for herself, for Max, and most of all for Samson.

Carole automatically folded herself into jumping position, her seat raised, her legs firm, and her arms steady. At just the right moment, Samson's hind legs flexed, propelling him up and forward. His forelegs tucked under him as they cleared the top rail, his head and neck stretched forward. A split second later, his forelegs touched down on the far side of the fence. Carole tensed slightly as they landed, half expecting to hear the clatter of rails coming down. But instead she heard a roar from the crowd. That was when she knew.

"Hi-ya!" she cried, spurring her horse forward. Samson galloped across the finish line, and only then did Carole dare to glance at the big clock over the judges' stand.

She let out a breath she hadn't even realized she was holding. They had made it under the time allowed. They had gone clear!

As Carole rode out of the ring after her round, Stevie decided it would probably seem unprofessional to scream out her friend's name and wave her hands over her head to get her attention and show how proud she was. So instead she satisfied herself with clapping until her hands hurt. She could hardly wait for the jump-off.

When Carole and Samson were out of sight and the next rider entered the ring, Stevie pushed her way through the crowd at the fence. There were still quite a few riders left to go, and Stevie wanted to find Phil and maybe Lisa and Callie and the others so that they could all watch the jump-off together.

The first person she found was Phil. Spotting him walking toward her between the rows of bleachers, she raced over to him and grabbed his hands excitedly. "Did you see Carole just now?" she cried. Then, realizing she hadn't seen her boyfriend since finishing her own dressage performance almost an hour earlier, she added, "Oh! Did you see me ride?"

"Didn't you hear me yelling your name from the audience?" Phil asked, squeezing her hands and then leaning in for a congratulatory kiss. "Of course I saw you. You were amazing!"

"Well, *sort of* amazing, maybe," Stevie admitted with a grin. "I mean, we weren't perfect or anything. We messed up one transition near the beginning, and Belle had a little trouble with that counter-canter today."

Phil waved his hands, as if shooing away a pesky fly. "I didn't even notice any of that stuff," he said loyally. "You looked perfect to me."

"Thanks." Stevie knew that he was just being nice, but she didn't mind. At the level of competition she and Belle had been up against, she knew that she had every reason to be pleased with their performance. She might not have ended up with a ribbon like George had—he'd taken the green sixth-place ribbon in the same event—but she knew that Max and the others would be proud of her, too. "Hey, speaking of perfection, did you see Carole's round just now?"

Phil nodded, looking impressed. "I can't believe she went clean," he said. "I mean, I always knew she was good. But after watching some of those other riders—you know, like Garrett Shanahan, and that dark-haired woman, what's her name . . ."

"I know." Stevie linked her arm through his as they made their way out of the bleachers to the relatively peaceful area behind the stands. "Carole really, you know, sort of fits in with that crowd." She shrugged. "Ben, too, actually. He was really good." Ben and Topside had ridden a few places before Carole, and they, too, had qualified for the jump-off.

Phil pulled her toward an empty bench under the shade of an evergreen tree. They sat down, and when he put his arm around her waist, Stevie leaned into his shoulder and breathed in the clean scent of soap from his shirt. It felt nice just relaxing, just being with Phil, after her exciting morning. She reminded herself to thank her parents for giving her the day off from her grounding. Maybe if she sounded grateful enough, she thought, they'd start thinking about lifting the punishment altogether.

She decided not to think about that. All she wanted to do was enjoy her day of freedom. "So are you having fun?" she asked without lifting her head from Phil's shoulder.

"Uh-huh." Phil paused. "I just wish I could have convinced A.J. to come today."

Stevie sat up and looked at him. "Me too," she said seriously. Phil's comment reminded her of the talk she'd had with Lisa the evening before. Stevie still could hardly believe that Lisa had seen A.J. drinking at a college bar. Lisa had sounded really worried, especially after Stevie had told her about what had happened on A.J.'s night out with Phil earlier in the week. As soon as she'd hung up with Lisa, Stevie had risked her parents' wrath by calling Phil immediately to tell him about the latest incident. But neither of them had had any ideas about what to do. The only thing they could agree on was that they had to do something before their friend got any further out of control.

Still, as concerned as she was about A.J., Stevie decided that figuring out how to help him could wait one more day. She and Phil couldn't do much for him as long as they were at the horse show, and worrying about it would only ruin their own day.

Instead, Stevie decided to focus on something a little more pleasant. "So my awesome gift for Carole is almost ready," she told Phil. "All I have to do is pick up the photos today after the show, decide which one to have blown up, and then pick that one up on Monday."

"That's great." Phil patted her knee. "Carole will love it, especially after the great job she and Samson are doing here today."

Stevie's eyes lit up. "Hey!" she said. "Maybe if she wins a ribbon, she can attach it to the frame somehow. Wouldn't that look—"

A friendly voice interrupted her. "Finally, some familiar faces!"

Looking up, Stevie saw Scott heading toward them with a smile on his handsome face. "Hi!" she called, standing up to greet him. "What have you been up to?"

Scott grinned. "Well, for one thing, I've been watching all my friends give brilliant performances in the ring," he said. "Congratulations, Stevie. You were great." He gave her a hug.

"Thanks," Stevie said, hugging him back. "We made some mistakes, but it was fun just to compete against all those awesome riders."

Phil laughed. "She's just being modest," he told Scott. "And believe me, that doesn't happen very often, so enjoy it while you can."

Stevie gave her boyfriend a playful punch on the shoulder. Then she glanced in the direction of the ring, which was hidden from their view at the moment, as a cheer went up from the crowd. "They'll be finished pretty soon," she commented. "We should try to find seats soon so that we have a good view of the jump-off. Where are Callie and Lisa?"

"The last time I saw Callie, she was still over at the pony rides with Maxi," Scott replied. "We probably shouldn't wait for her."

"What about Lisa?" Phil asked. "I haven't seen her all day."

Scott shrugged. "She was supposed to catch a ride over with Red."

"Wait," Stevie said. "What was the deal with her again? Why didn't she come with you guys?"

"Oh, didn't Callie tell you?" Scott shrugged again. "I'm really not too clear on the whole story. Callie talked to Red about it. I think it had something to do with Prancer. Lisa wanted to stick around to take care of her until the vet got there to check on her. Or something like that."

"The vet?" Stevie felt a sudden pang of concern. As far as she knew, Judy Barker hadn't scheduled a checkup for Prancer that day. Of course, she wasn't sure that she hadn't, either. Maybe Red had asked Judy to stop by for an extra visit. "Is something wrong? What did Red say?"

"Sorry, I really don't know." Scott spread his hands helplessly. "Callie's the one who spoke to him. All I know is that Lisa didn't ride over with us, but she and Red were supposed to come over later."

Phil grabbed Stevie's hand and squeezed it, obviously recognizing the worried look on her face. "Don't panic," he said gently. "This place is a zoo. I'm sure Lisa's here somewhere and we just haven't seen her yet. And I'm sure Prancer's perfectly fine."

"Okay." Stevie did her best to believe him, especially since she knew he was probably right. The show grounds were so crowded that Stevie had only caught one glimpse of her parents watching her dressage round from the front row of the stands, and she hadn't seen her brothers at all. Lisa was there somewhere. It was silly to get worked up over nothing on such a wonderful day. "Then we'd better not wait for her, either," she told the two guys. "Let's grab some seats up high, where we can see the ring and also keep a lookout for Lisa and Callie."

Every time the crowd cheered at the end of another round, Carole glanced toward the main ring from the warm-up area. She was walking Samson slowly around and around, trying to keep him alert and limber. By her estimation, there couldn't be more than two or three riders left to go before it would be time for the jump-off.

I can't believe this is happening, she thought joyfully, glancing at the big black horse beside her. He seemed to understand that they weren't finished yet. His expression was eager, and he hardly seemed tired at all after the strenuous first round. *I can't believe I'm really here, waiting to go back into the ring with these people.*

She cast a quick glance around at the other riders in the practice ring. Only five others had qualified for the jump-off so far, including Garrett Shanahan and a couple of other well-known competitors.

Most exciting of all, though, was that Ben had made it, too. Carole glanced across the warm-up

224

ring to where Ben was walking Topside, suddenly feeling a swell of pride to be a part of the great team of Pine Hollow riders. At that moment Ben turned and caught her looking at him. Instead of scowling or looking suspicious, he actually lifted one hand in a sort of half wave. Then he turned Topside and came toward her, leading the bay gelding, who looked almost as fresh as Samson.

"Nice job out there, Ben," Carole told him sincerely when he was close enough to hear. "You and Topside were really good."

"You too," Ben replied gruffly. Carole wasn't sure, but she thought she caught a glimpse of pleasure, or maybe pride, in his dark eyes.

"Thanks. It was all thanks to Samson. He's really on today, and he—" Carole broke off. She'd suddenly spotted her father standing in the crowd that was pressing up against the rail marking off the path between the warm-up area and the main ring. He was looking her way, so she grinned and waved, giving him a thumbs-up with her free hand.

Colonel Hanson saw her and waved back. But Carole couldn't help noticing that he didn't return her smile—in fact, his expression was rather grim. *That's weird*, she thought fleetingly. *Who would have guessed that Dad would be more nervous than I am?*

The truth was, she didn't feel very nervous at all. As far as she was concerned, she and Samson had already proved themselves. They had shown everyone that they deserved to be there, competing against the top horses and riders on the East Coast. Who knew where they could go from here? The future seemed limitless, full of all sorts of exciting possibilities. Carole couldn't wait for the jump-off.

Carole was scheduled to ride fifth out of the six riders in the jump-off. Only Garrett Shanahan would follow her, which would give her a pretty good idea of what she had to beat.

"It's almost time, big guy," she told Samson, ignoring the sound of the announcer explaining the rules of the jump-off to the audience.

Just then Denise appeared at her side. "Hi, Carole," she said. "How are you feeling?"

"Great," Carole replied truthfully. "I can't wait for my turn!"

Denise smiled. "Good. I just came over to see if you want me to watch Samson while you check out the competition."

"That would be great!" Carole said gratefully. "Thanks, Denise." Handing over Samson's lead, she hurried toward the fence. Now she would really be able to see what she was up against.

The first rider was clearly nervous as she entered the ring, and it rubbed off on her horse. The pair brought down two rails out of the first three. They ended up with a good time but far too many jumping faults.

Ben rode second. His face held its usual impassive expression as he aimed Topside at the first fence in the shortened jump-off course. Carole crossed her fingers, hoping they would do well. For most of the course, they did. Topside handled each obstacle in his usual controlled, professional manner. But when there were just two fences left, Carole saw Ben glance quickly at the clock. She could guess what was going through his head. They were clean so far, but they were being so careful that their time was moderate at best. With four riders to go after them, they couldn't afford to post a time that would be easy to beat.

Watching closely, Carole saw Ben urge Topside on faster. The plan backfired. They were too rushed approaching the next obstacle. Ben saw it, too, and he did his best to correct it. Topside tried valiantly to adjust his stride as his rider was asking. But there just wasn't enough time. The bay gelding met the fence at an awkward angle, and though he struggled to leap up and over anyway, his front hooves clipped the top rail and brought it clattering to the ground.

Carole's heart went out to Ben. She knew how

disappointed he must be. But it didn't show on his face. It also didn't show in his riding. He collected Topside, steadying him after the mistake, and aimed him toward the next and last obstacle. They cleared it easily and galloped across the finish line with a respectable time.

Well, he's guaranteed fifth place at least, Carole thought as she watched her teammate ride out of the ring, seeming oblivious to the applause of the crowd as he patted Topside's sweaty neck and whispered to the horse. *Maybe better. Sometimes that kind of solid, low-fault performance is enough to win a competition like this.*

As if proving her thoughts true, the next two competitors each brought down two fences. As Carole hurried to meet Denise, who was leading Samson toward her, she knew that Ben's ride was the one she had to beat so far. All she had to do was go clear in a decent amount of time, and the win was hers.

Not allowing herself to think about or even glance at Garrett Shanahan, who was already mounted on his big chestnut mare and waiting quietly on the far side of the warm-up ring, Carole quickly mounted and rode Samson toward the main ring. She knew she should probably be feeling nervous, but instead she was strangely calm. Anything could happen out there, of course, and Carole knew better than to be overconfident. One little mistake, one misstep or un-luckily placed stone on the ground, could mean a fault. But despite all that, it was hard to be too worried when she was riding a horse like Samson.

As the starting bell rang, Carole's mind snapped into focus. All she could see was the fences in front of her, the packed ground leading up to each one. All she could hear was Samson's breathing and the thud of his hooves on the dirt. They soared easily over one fence, then another. Samson was moving fast, but Carole was still in complete control, guiding the sharp turns between obstacles and measuring each stride to keep them on track. Another fence flashed under them, then another, and several more. Before she knew it, they were crossing the finish line with the first clean round in the jump-off!

"Samson! We did it!" Carole whispered glee-fully, leaning forward to pat her horse even as she glanced up at the timer over the judges' stand. She blinked, not quite believing her eyes. She and Samson had beaten the next fastest time by more than two full seconds!

The wild cheers from the crowd finally broke through, and Carole grinned. Turning in the saddle, she waved at the stands, hoping that her friends and her father were out there somewhere watching her.

Garrett Shanahan was waiting near the entrance for his turn. Carole blushed as she saw him looking at her with a slight smile on his handsome face. She blushed even more as he touched his crop to his hard hat, nodding as she rode past. She waved self-consciously and called "good luck," though she wasn't sure whether he could hear her over the roar of the crowd that was still cheering her clear round.

Denise was waiting to help her dismount. "That was incredible, Carole!" she said excitedly. "You're in first place!"

"Thanks." Carole glanced toward the ring at the sound of the starting horn. "I guess we'll get second, at least."

"Go watch Garrett," Denise urged. "I'll walk Samson."

Carole hesitated, torn between taking care of her horse and watching Garrett's ride. But then she nodded and raced back toward the fence. The clapping from the crowd told her that Garret must have cleared his first fence. She was just in time to see his approach to the second, which was flawless. The chestnut soared up and over easily, her hooves barely seeming to touch the ground on the other side before she was off and running toward the next obstacle.

With her heart in her mouth, Carole watched the rest of the round. As much as she wanted to win—to see the judges clip that blue ribbon onto Samson's bridle, the first of many they would surely be winning together—she couldn't quite bring herself to wish for Garrett and his mare to make a mistake. They were so beautiful to watch in action that Carole found herself cheering after each fence along with the rest of the spectators. It was only after the chestnut had cleared the final obstacle that Carole realized what it meant. Garrett had gone clear, too.

She already felt a twinge of disappointment as she glanced automatically toward the time clock. But then she gasped as she saw the numbers flashing there. Garrett's time was excellent, but hers and Samson's was still half a second faster. She had won!

The next few minutes passed in a blur. Carole raced back to tell Denise the news. They both hugged Samson, who seemed a little confused by all the excitement. Then Max and Ben and George were there, too, hugging and congratulating her.

Sometime during all the joyful commotion, Garrett Shanahan walked past the group, leading his mare. Carole looked over just in time to catch his eye. The older rider looked tired and a bit disappointed, but he was smiling at her.

"Nice riding, young lady," he called. "Congratulations."

"Thanks," Carole replied shyly. "You too."

Garrett nodded and glanced at Samson. "That's quite a horse," he said. "Looks like I made a good decision."

Carole wasn't sure what he meant by that, but she just smiled politely. She knew that under ordinary circumstances she would be thrilled that a famous rider like Garrett Shanahan was even speaking to her. But these were no ordinary circumstances.

I can't believe I won! she thought gleefully as Garrett moved on and more people came over to congratulate her. *This really is the best day of my life!*

FOURTEEN

Carole couldn't take her eyes off the blue ribbon fluttering from Samson's bridle. It seemed to represent everything she had planned for the two of them. After all, this was only the beginning. Soon Samson would be hers—all hers, forever. Who knew what the two of them could accomplish together?

"Congratulations!" Stevie shrieked, racing up as Carole led her horse out of the ring. "You were awesome!" She grabbed Carole in a tight hug.

Carole laughed breathlessly, wriggling free. "Thanks," she said. "But you should be hugging Samson. He's the one who did most of the work."

Stevie obliged, throwing her arms around the big black horse despite his sweaty coat. Then she stepped back and held out her hand. "Let me take him," she told Carole. "I'll start cooling him out for you. I'm sure you want to take a few

233

minutes to bask in the admiration of your adoring fans."

"Well, okay. Thanks." Carole wanted to take care of Samson herself, give him a good grooming to thank him for his incredible effort, but she figured that could wait a few minutes. First she wanted to find her father and make sure he'd seen her win. That could be the first step in convincing him that she and Samson were meant to be together.

As she left the warm-up area, Carole was a little surprised to discover that Stevie hadn't been totally kidding about her fans. Everyone she passed seemed to want to speak to her, to pat her on the back or congratulate her. One little girl even asked Carole to autograph her show program. Carole obliged, though she couldn't help feeling embarrassed and slightly foolish as she signed her name.

Still, she had to admit that it was fun being the center of attention. It was almost like being a celebrity, at least for the moment. Before long Carole found herself nodding and smiling and waving to complete strangers as naturally as if she'd been doing it all her life. She also encountered a few faces she knew in the throngs of people surrounding her—friends from school, younger riders from Pine Hollow, neighbors from her street. Even one of the waitresses from

TD's yelled out, "Way to go, horse girl!" as Carole walked past.

It took her a while to find her father in the crowd. But at last she spotted him standing near the grandstand entrance.

"Dad!" she cried, waving and racing toward him. "There you are. Did you see?"

Colonel Hanson nodded and leaned forward to plant a kiss on her forehead. "I saw. Good riding, Carole. Congratulations."

"Thanks." Carole grinned and glanced around. "Can you believe the way everybody's so excited for me? Isn't it great?"

"It's very nice. It was an exciting contest."

For the first time, Carole noticed that her father's smile looked strained. And his voice sounded rather odd, too. "Is something wrong, Dad?" she asked. "You look kind of weird. Is anything the matter?"

Her father hesitated. "Well," he said after a moment, clearing his throat. His forehead creased into a frown. "I was going to wait until we had some privacy. But maybe this can't wait after all."

He gestured for her to follow him around the back of the stands to a quiet spot behind an empty concession stand. She did so, feeling puzzled and slightly deflated. What was going on?

When they were more or less alone, Colonel

Hanson continued. "I just found out something—something you've been keeping from me, Carole. And I have to say, as proud as I am of what you've accomplished today, I'm feeling pretty furious with you right now."

For a second Carole was sure he'd found out somehow about her deal with Tanya. She gulped. Had Stevie or Lisa let something slip? Or had Tanya called their house again? "Um, yes?" she said uncertainly, trying to buy more time to figure out how to explain her decision. She was a little surprised that his first response was anger. Her father was pretty even-tempered—she would have expected surprise, maybe disbelief or concern. But there was no mistaking his expression. "What is it, Dad?"

He crossed his arms over his chest. "I went over to say hello to your teachers after you pointed them out earlier," he said evenly. "While I was chatting with your history teacher, Ms. Shepard, she asked me if I was feeling better these days. At first I wasn't sure what she was talking about."

Carole felt her heart freeze. She remembered the lie she had told her history teacher—pretending that her father had been seriously ill as an excuse for failing that test all those weeks ago. "Oh," she said weakly, wondering how much of

236

the truth her father and her teacher had figured out.

Colonel Hanson didn't keep her in suspense for long. "It took us a few minutes, but then we realized what had happened." His expression was severe. "You lied to your teacher. You took advantage of her trust and her kind nature by making up a story as an excuse for not studying. You told her I was sick and that's why you did poorly on your test."

"I'm sorry. I really don't know why I told her that," Carole blurted out, feeling overwhelmed by the guilt she had kept down for so long, which now burst out of her. "I guess it was just that I knew if I flunked that test, Max wouldn't let me ride until I brought my grade up, and—well, anyway, I've spent the past month feeling horrible about it, especially the cheating part."

"Cheating part?" Colonel Hanson repeated sharply, his expression darkening even more. "Which part would that be, exactly?"

Carole gulped, wondering why she could never seem to control her mouth. Obviously her father and Ms. Shepard hadn't gotten past her lie. They hadn't realized what else she had done that fateful week to save her grade and her riding privileges.

"What cheating part?" Colonel Hanson said

again when Carole didn't answer. "I'm waiting, Carole."

"Nothing," she said quickly, wishing desperately that she could rewind the past few minutes of her life and avoid this whole conversation. She grabbed a wooden pillar on the back of the empty concession stand for support. "I meant lying. Not cheating."

Her father frowned. "I'm going to ask you once more, Carole, and I expect a truthful answer. Is there anything more you want to share about this incident?"

Suddenly Carole gave up. It was too late. Her wonderful day had already gone dark and horrible, and all because of something she'd done ages ago, something she'd been sure was behind her. It was no use trying to hide it anymore. She couldn't stand lying to her father for one more second. "Yes," she said, her voice shaking. "I wish I'd told you a long time ago. I—I didn't study enough for the retest Ms. Shepard gave me, either. So when she left the room . . ." She swallowed hard.

"Yes?" Colonel Hanson prompted grimly.

Carole didn't dare meet his eye. "I kind of, um, peeked at some of the answers in my textbook," she said quietly. "I know it was wrong. I couldn't believe I'd done it afterward. But it was too late by then."

Colonel Hanson didn't answer for a long, tense moment. When he spoke again, his voice was dangerously calm. "I'm leaving the horse show and driving home now," he said. "I realize that you have a duty to help Max bring the horses back safely, and I expect you to fulfill that duty. But as soon as you're finished, I want you home to discuss this."

Carole blinked, hardly believing her ears. She didn't know what she'd been expecting, but it wasn't merely an order to come home and talk about what she'd done. For a second, she dared to hope that she might get off easy this time. After all, it was the first time she'd ever done anything so horrible and wrong. Surely her father realized that, too. "Okay, Dad," she said quickly. "I promise. I'll be there as soon as I can."

Colonel Hanson nodded and started to turn away. Then he paused. "Oh, and one more thing," he said coldly. "Before you leave Pine Hollow, you might as well tell Max he'll have to find a replacement for your job there. And you'd better speak to him about finding someone to exercise Starlight for you, too. Because after today, you won't be setting foot in that stable for a good long time—the rest of the semester at the very least. You're grounded."

Judy Barker shook her head, her face twisting into a grimace of sorrow. "I can't pick it up at all anymore," she said, lowering her stethoscope from Prancer's flank. "I think we've lost the second foal, too."

Red glanced at his watch, his face somber. "I could try reaching Max again," he offered.

"Don't bother." Judy sighed and rubbed her eyes with the balls of her hands. "It would just make him worry. There's nothing he could do anyway."

Lisa wished she could shove her fingers in her ears so that she wouldn't have to hear any more bad news. She and Red and Judy had been with Prancer all day, and things just kept getting worse. The mare was in obvious distress, her sides heaving and her head hanging lower than ever. Judy had given her antibiotics and something for the pain, but she admitted there wasn't much else she could do except wait and see what happened.

Walking to Prancer's head, Lisa ran her fingers across the mare's cheek. Her mind was struggling with the idea that Prancer might not make it. It just didn't seem possible—not now, when the mare was finally going to be all hers.

Lisa's eyes filled with tears as she looked at the horse she'd loved for so long. Prancer hardly seemed aware of her presence. She was staring

240

blankly, all her efforts apparently focused on breathing through her suffering.

No, it didn't seem possible. And it definitely didn't seem fair.

Carole was in shock as she stumbled back to the stable area. Her mind was reeling with her father's pronouncement. Despite her protests, he had remained firm. She was grounded, and that meant no friends, no phone calls, no TV—and no Pine Hollow.

He can't do this to me, Carole thought as she flashed her badge at the woman guarding the gate to the stable area. *He can't possibly mean it. He's just angry right now, not thinking straight. . . . He knows what Pine Hollow, my job there, means to me!*

Even as she thought it, though, she knew she was kidding herself. Her father didn't hand out punishments lightly, and he didn't make empty threats. Like the good Marine he'd always been, he always followed through on his word. If he said she was banned from Pine Hollow, she was banned.

Still, Carole couldn't quite make herself believe it. It was too horrible, too foreign a concept. What would she do with her time if she couldn't go to the stable? She couldn't even imagine. Horses and riding had always been such a huge part of her life that she couldn't picture the days without them.

On top of all that, she was still having trouble realizing that her dirty little secret was out in the open at last. She thought she'd been so careful, so lucky in keeping anyone from knowing what she'd done. But soon everyone would know what she was—a cheater, a liar, an awful person.

She tried not to think about that. First she had to figure out how to handle things right now. What was she going to say to Max about her job, about Starlight's departure that very evening? More importantly, her plans to buy Samson from Max suddenly looked a whole lot more difficult, if not impossible. How was she going to ask her father for money now? How was she going to convince Max to sell her the big black gelding when she wasn't even allowed near the stable?

It was all so overwhelming that she couldn't stand it. She figured the only thing that might help her make sense of it all was seeing Samson himself. Maybe just being with the horse she loved so much, taking strength from him, would help her figure things out—or at least make her feel a little better.

She headed for the Pine Hollow stable area. When she arrived, she saw that Max had taken over Samson's care from Stevie, who had disappeared. Max was walking the big gelding back and forth up the path, cooling him out carefully. Walking alongside him was Garrett Shanahan.

Carole was surprised to see the famous rider hanging out with Max again, but she didn't have the energy to wonder about that at the moment. She just wanted to lead Samson off somewhere private and wrap her arms around his neck for a while until the numb feeling in her brain wore off and she could think straight again.

Mustering as normal an expression as she could manage, she hurried toward the two men and the horse. "Hi," she said, willing herself to sound cheerful, like a girl who'd just won a blue ribbon instead of one whose whole world was collapsing. "Um, thanks for taking care of Samson for me, Max. I can take him now."

Max obviously hadn't seen her approaching. "Oh!" he said, and brought Samson to a halt. "Carole."

Garrett Shanahan stepped toward her and stuck out his hand. "Congratulations again on your win," he said cordially. "You rode very well. You deserved the blue. So did your horse—or perhaps I should say *my* horse." He smiled and winked at Max, looking pleased, then reached out to pat Samson on the neck.

Carole frowned, not sure what he meant. Glancing at Max for help, she saw that his face had gone white under his tan. "Carole," he said. "I was going to tell you after the show. I—uh, I didn't want to break your concentration by saying anything about this before." He shrugged. "Besides, Garrett and I didn't really finalize the deal until this morning, so . . ."

Carole struggled to follow his words. What was he telling her? Her mind suddenly seemed to be moving like molasses, though she wasn't sure why.

Garrett chuckled, clapping Max on the shoulder. "That's right," he said. "Wily old Max here knew what he had even before today's performance. He kept me bargaining for almost a month—ever since a friend of mine first told me about Samson here."

"But—" Carole clenched her fists so hard that her fingernails dug into her palms. She couldn't be hearing what she thought she was hearing. "Do you mean you—Max, did you—Is Samson—"

"I'm thrilled to have such a wonderful new horse to work with," Garrett said, still apparently unaware of Carole's distress. He was gazing happily at Samson. "I've been looking for a good prospect ever since I retired my favorite horse, Cloverleaf, a while back. And now I'm pretty sure I've found a new favorite in Samson. I think we'll make quite a team, if I do say so myself."

A sharp stab pierced Carole's heart as she realized the truth at last. Max had sold Samson. The horse of her dreams would be going far away, all the way to Canada, where someone else would ride him and train him and take care of him and love him. Carole hadn't felt a pain like that since her mother had died all those years ago. It was so strong that she wasn't sure she could bear it without shattering into a million brittle, anguished pieces.

"Um, I'll walk him for you now," she mumbled, grabbing blindly at the lead rope through a sheen of tears. Any second now they would spill over and she wouldn't be able to stop them. Before that happened, she wanted to get away from the men, away from everyone except Samson.

Max seemed to understand. Shooting her a look of sympathy and concern, he handed over the lead and then turned to steer Garrett away, saying something about a cup of coffee. Carole didn't stick around to hear any more. Turning a startled Samson around quickly, she headed for a copse of trees behind the row of trailers.

She was just about cried out half an hour later, though the ache in her soul had only grown deeper. Samson had settled down to graze in a patch of grass behind the clump of brush where Carole was hiding.

She sat on the ground with her head buried in her arms, wondering how this had happened. Her wonderful world had been blown away completely, and she couldn't see any way of getting it back. Everything she cared about was gone. Starlight. Her job at Pine Hollow. And Samson. The more she thought about it, the deeper her despair.

"Carole?" she heard Ben say from close by, snapping her out of her thoughts.

She raised her face from her hands and blinked at him through the glaze of her tears. "Ben?" she said thickly. "What are you doing here? I want to be alone. Go away."

He ignored her command, instead lowering himself to the grass at her side. Glancing at Samson, he cleared his throat. "Max told me."

Those three little words made the tears well up again. Swiping at her eyes with her hand, Carole swallowed hard. "I didn't know until just now," she said, her words wobbly and uncertain. "I had no idea."

"Me either." Ben shifted his weight awkwardly as if trying to find a comfortable position on the hard ground. "He didn't tell anyone."

"But why?" Carole leaned a little closer to Ben, gazing at him beseechingly. Maybe if she figured out how this had happened, it would all start to make some sense. "Why didn't he tell us he was thinking of . . ." She broke off and glanced over at Samson again, who continued to graze, unperturbed by their conversation.

Ben shrugged. "Don't know. I guess maybe he wasn't sure. Anyway, uh—I'm, you know, sorry."

Carole nodded, but she couldn't answer. The tears that she'd thought were played out were returning with a vengeance, filling her eyes and spilling over.

Ben looked uneasy. "I'm sorry," he said again. "Uh, I shouldn't have said—I was just trying to tell you. I understand what you're going through. You know." He reached over and patted her clumsily on the shoulder.

Not trusting her voice to answer him, to tell him it wasn't his fault, she responded by letting out another sob and clinging to his arm. Right then Ben was the only one who might possibly understand how utterly and completely miserable she was. Besides that, he was a link to Pine Hollow and the life she had just lost. She didn't want to scare him off.

With a startled cough, Ben let her pull him close. He even put his other arm around her, patting her softly on the back. "It's okay," he murmured huskily. "It's okay."

Carole squeezed her eyes shut tight and collapsed against the solid, comforting warmth of his body. Even through her agony, she noticed that he smelled good—like hay and leather and horse sweat. That snapped her out of her heartache long enough for her to realize for the first time just how unusual this situation was. Suddenly she was very aware of Ben's arms around her, of his warm breath on her forehead. She could feel his heart beating in his chest as she clutched him to her.

Feeling shy and a bit ashamed at letting him see her so desperate and out of control, she pulled back slightly and looked up at him. "Sorry," she said with a self-conscious sniffle. "I didn't mean to—um, this is weird. Us like this, I mean."

Ben gazed back at her, his eyes uncertain. For a long moment, he didn't answer. But he didn't pull away either, as Carole had expected him to do at the first opportunity. Instead, his arms tightened slightly. Before she knew what was happening, Carole saw his face moving slowly toward her own. She held her breath, not sure how to respond, but unable to look away from those dark, searching eyes.

A few seconds later, their lips met. And for the moment, at least, Carole forgot about everything else.

FIFTEEN

"Poor Carole." Callie shook her head sympathetically and balanced on her crutches as Stevie swung open Pine Hollow's main doors later that afternoon. "Did she have any idea Max was planning to sell Samson?"

"No way." Stevie bit her lip as she thought about how drastically Carole's wonderful day had changed. She felt awful for her. It was bad enough that Colonel Hanson had found out that Carole had cheated on some test at school—Stevie herself was still shocked by that one, since Carole was generally one of the most honest people she knew—but it didn't seem fair that on the very same day, she would find out that all her hopes and plans to buy Samson were ruined. "I don't think anyone knew about that."

Callie sighed. "It's a shame," she said. "Especially after she and Samson did so well today. It's too bad she didn't at least have time to enjoy her blue ribbon for a while."

Stevie had to agree with that. "So much for my birthday present for her," she murmured, thinking of the half-finished project in her room at home. There was no way she would ever give it to Carole now.

Seeing Callie's curious look, Stevie quickly explained her plan for Carole's birthday as the two girls wandered toward the tack room, where Belle's dirty saddle and bridle were waiting. Callie had agreed to baby-sit Maxi and Mini that evening while Max and Deborah took a well-deserved rest together after their respective busy weeks. Maxi was riding home from the show with Max, who hadn't arrived yet, so Callie was hanging out with Stevie while she waited for them.

"It's a shame," Callie said again when Stevie had finished her story. "She and Samson were quite a pair." She shrugged. "I guess she'll have to go back to riding Starlight in shows now, huh? Even if he's not quite up to Samson's standards, he's still a pretty good jumper."

Stevie gulped as one more horrible fact hit her with the force of a freight train. Tonight was the night Starlight was leaving Pine Hollow for his new home with Tanya. With everything else that was happening, she had almost forgotten about that. She felt her heart breaking on her friend's behalf. Soon Carole would be left with nothing at all.

She and Callie had almost reached the locker room when they heard someone calling their names. Turning, Stevie saw Lisa walking toward them, her face hidden by shadows.

"Hey," Stevie said accusingly, suddenly remembering that she hadn't seen Lisa at the show. "What happened to you today? Didn't you . . ."

Her voice trailed off as Lisa came closer and Stevie got her first good look at her friend's face. Lisa's expression was bleak, her eyes red-rimmed. She looked discouraged, sorrowful, and completely exhausted.

"Lisa?" Stevie said uncertainly. "What—What's wrong?"

"It's Prancer," Lisa replied blankly. "Judy's been here all day."

"Prancer?" Stevie repeated, her earlier worries rushing back at full force. She exchanged glances with Callie, then turned back to Lisa. "What's the matter with her?"

Lisa shrugged, and for a second Stevie didn't think she was going to answer. But then she sighed and spoke. "You'd better come see her now. I think she's dying."

Carole managed to slip into the stable building without encountering anyone, leaving Denise and George to unload the horses. She didn't want to have to talk to anybody at the moment. There were too many confused feelings rattling around inside her. Now that she was back, she couldn't put off her thoughts of Starlight any longer. Tanya would be there soon to pick him up, and then Carole would have to face up to life without any special horse to share it with at all. Not Samson, and not Starlight, either.

Heading for the office, Carole dropped her stable key into the top desk drawer. She wouldn't be needing it for a while. She still wasn't sure how she was going to explain things to Max—she was just glad that she'd ended up riding back to Willow Creek with Denise and George, who had tactfully avoided all mention of Samson and chatted with each other about their own events the whole way home. Carole wasn't ready to face Max just yet. And she certainly wasn't ready to face Ben.

Her heart thumped once at the thought of him. What had that kiss meant? Thinking back, she couldn't even quite recall how it had happened. Which of them had started moving toward the other first? She wasn't sure, but she knew that the kiss itself had been wonderful. Ben hadn't said a word, but after their lips had finally parted, he had stared at her with the strangest, stunned look on his face. Jumping to his feet, he had mumbled something about helping Max and then rushed off, leaving Carole feeling dazed and flustered.

As she blinked, trying to guess what that expression in his eyes could have meant, Carole noticed that the light on the office answering machine was blinking. Automatically, she punched the Play button and reached for a pad of paper and a pen. Realizing what she was doing, she gulped at how ingrained her job had become.

The machine clicked on, and the message poured out. "Hi!" a cheerful voice chirped. "This message is for Carole Hanson. Carole, it's Tanya. I tried calling you at home, but no one answered, so I figured I'd try here. I just wanted to let you know that I won't be buying Starlight after all. Daddy and I just got back from a stable he heard about where they're selling a Hanoverian, and we think a well-bred European-type horse like that would be much better for me than a regular old American horse like Starlight. Sorry about the late notice and everything, but, well, you know. Good luck with finding another buyer. Bye!"

The machine beeped and continued to the next message, which was from the local feed company, but Carole just stared at the pad in her hand in complete shock. Had she heard right? Was Tanya really backing out of their deal?

Before she knew what she was doing, she was reaching for the phone and dialing Tanya's home number. After a few rings, Mrs. Appel picked up. When she heard why Carole was calling, she gave a meek, slightly sheepish laugh.

"I hope this doesn't cause you too many problems," she told Carole in her soft, tentative voice. "Our Tanya can be impulsive, but I'm afraid her heart is set on this other horse now."

"Really?" Carole clutched the phone tighter. "So she definitely doesn't want to buy Starlight anymore?"

"That's right," the woman replied. "I'm very sorry. But my husband was quite firm about the deal not being final because no money was exchanged, and so—"

"Okay," Carole said. "I mean, that's fine. I'm not going to argue or anything. I just wanted to make sure." She hung up the phone and stared at it. She could hardly believe that Tanya had changed her mind so casually, especially when she'd been so excited about picking up Starlight that very day. Buying a horse was an important decision, and the fact that Tanya was obviously taking it so lightly was a sure sign that she wasn't worthy of a good horse like Starlight. Carole could only hope the owner of that Hanoverian knew what he was doing.

But she couldn't manage to feel too upset about Tanya's careless change of heart. In fact, right at the moment it seemed like the only bright spot in her horrible afternoon. *Well*, she thought a bit bashfully, her mind flashing back to the moment Ben's surprisingly tender lips had found her own, *it's one of the only bright spots*.

She hurried out of the office, heading for Starlight's stall, suddenly eager to see him. The gelding was looking out over the half door when she approached. He nickered when he spotted her, and Carole couldn't help smiling. "Hey, boy," she said softly as she let herself into the stall and ran her hands over her horse's smooth face and neck, pausing to scratch all his favorite spots. Starlight snorted and shoved his big head into her chest, obviously hoping for some treats. "Sorry, I don't have anything for you today," she told him. "But I'll be sure to bring lots of carrots and apple pieces the next time I . . ." Her voice trailed off as she realized what she'd been about to say: *the next time I come*. When would that be? Unless she could convince her father to change his mind, it would be a long, long time.

Carole's knees felt weak at the thought, and she slid down the wall onto the soft, prickly mat of straw on the floor. How was she going to survive without Pine Hollow for so long? At the thought, some of her other problems came creeping back, overtaking her relief that Starlight was still hers. How was she going to say good-bye to Samson? It hurt even to think about it. She'd been so sure that they were meant to be together. And now . . .

The sound of approaching voices interrupted her thoughts. Standing up, she glanced out and saw Callie walking down the aisle. Maxi was with her, her small hand tucked into Callie's larger one, chattering away about the pony rides and the horse show in general.

Callie spotted Carole looking out at them. "There you are!" she exclaimed, interrupting Maxi's flow of words and hurrying toward Starlight's stall. "The others were looking for you."

"Others?" Carole repeated blankly.

"Lisa and Stevie," Callie explained. "They're with Prancer. She's running a really high fever, and Lisa says she's been getting worse all day. It doesn't look good."

Carole gasped. *"Prancer!"* she cried. "What do you mean? What's wrong?"

Callie shook her head grimly, shooting a quick glance at Maxi. "You'd better go check it out for yourself."

Carole guessed that she didn't want to say too much in front of the little girl. That meant it had to be pretty bad. Her heart in her throat, she let herself out of the stall and rushed toward the other main row of stalls, where Prancer lived.

What could have happened to Prancer in one day? she wondered worriedly. She gulped as a thought occurred to her. *Or did something happen sooner? Did we—I—not notice she wasn't feeling well because I was so wrapped up in getting ready for the show?* Even the idea made her feel guilty.

As she rounded the corner, she almost ran smack into Ben, who was coming the other way. "Oh!" Carole cried, startled. "Um, sorry." She felt herself blushing furiously. She hadn't seen Ben face-to-face since their kiss, and now she wasn't sure what to say to him. "I mean, uh, hi."

"Hi," Ben replied curtly. He didn't meet her eye. "Excuse me." He stepped aside and hurried on past her without a second glance.

Carole gulped, feeling as though she'd been slapped. What was going on? Ben had acted as if nothing at all had happened between them. No, she realized, turning to stare after him, it was even worse than that. He'd acted as if he *wished* nothing had happened. She might not have much experience with guys, but she wasn't completely stupid. She knew what it meant when a guy kissed you one minute and looked straight through you the next.

Her eyes welled with hot tears, but she forced

them down angrily. She didn't have time to worry about Ben. She had to find her friends, to see what was going on with Prancer. Later she could figure out how to deal with this horrible new problem in her horrible life.

"I can't believe it." Stevie was stunned by what Lisa and Carole had just told her. She leaned back against the wall of Prancer's stall, trying to take it in. "Your dad was going to buy her for you?" She looked at Lisa.

Lisa nodded, her face haggard. She glanced at Prancer, who was lying on the straw nearby, her sides heaving as she struggled for each breath. "It was going to be a surprise," she said softly. "I'm not sure, but I think he was probably going to tell me about it over Thanksgiving."

Stevie couldn't answer. Putting her hand over her mouth, she gazed at Prancer mournfully. *It's not fair*, she thought, tears springing to her eyes as she watched Prancer lie there, dulled by the medicine Judy had given her as well as by her own pain. *Lisa has loved Prancer for years. And she's always wanted her own horse. How can it be that now, just when Prancer was about to become hers . . .*

She couldn't finish the thought. It was too tragic to bear. She reached for Lisa's hand and squeezed it, hoping that her friend knew how deeply she felt for her. Glancing at Carole, she saw that her red-rimmed eyes were focused on Lisa. For the moment, at least, she seemed to have forgotten her own considerable problems.

Judy poked her head over the stall door and looked in at the three girls somberly. "How's she doing?" the vet asked.

Lisa shook her head and swallowed hard. "Not good," she said, loosening her hand from Stevie's grip and running her hands over Prancer's side. The mare didn't even seem to notice her touch.

Max appeared beside Judy. He looked grim. "I hate to say this, girls," he said, his voice gruff and sad. "But I think it's time."

Stevie immediately understood what he meant. "Are you sure?" she asked. "But what if—" She broke off when she saw the look on Judy's face. That was all the answer she needed. The vet didn't think there was any chance that Prancer would pull through this. All they could do for her now was to end her suffering quickly and humanely rather than letting her pain continue any longer.

Stevie gulped and looked over at her friends. Both of them had gone pale, but neither said a word. Stevie returned her gaze to Max and Judy. "Is it all right if we stay with her?" she asked, knowing it was what her friends would want.

Judy nodded. She disappeared for a moment, and Stevie heard the sounds of the vet snapping open her bag and preparing her equipment. Glancing at Lisa and Carole, she saw that they heard it, too. Stevie wished there was something she could do to ease the tortured expression on Lisa's face. As hard as it was for Stevie and Carole to see Prancer like this, she knew it was hardest of all for Lisa. Lisa had loved her more than any of them. She had ridden her countless times, in shows and exhibitions, on trail rides and in riding classes. For years now, they had been a pair. And now, just when Lisa should be looking forward to having the amiable, sweet-tempered Thoroughbred all to herself at last, Prancer was being yanked cruelly away from her. Stevie didn't know how she could stand it.

She cleared her throat and touched Lisa gently on the arm. "Do you want us to leave you alone with her for a minute?"

Lisa shook her head. "No, please stay," she said, her voice choked. "I think we should all be here for this."

All too soon, Judy entered the stall, holding a hypodermic needle. "Are you ready?" she asked the girls.

"Just a second." Carole scooted forward to Prancer's head. Lifting it onto her lap, she hugged the mare tightly for a moment, murmuring a few words that Stevie couldn't hear.

When she was finished, Stevie moved forward and hugged Prancer herself. The mare didn't protest or try to move away. Her head and neck felt heavy as Stevie wrapped her arms around her, and the only sound the horse made was the rasp of her breathing.

"Good-bye, Prancer," Stevie whispered into the mare's limp ear. "We'll miss you. You've been such a—a good, fine horse. Good-bye." Her voice cracked on the last words, and she felt tears trickling down her face. Too choked up to say anything more, she put what she was feeling into one last hug before lowering the mare's head carefully to the straw again and moving aside.

By wordless agreement, Stevie and Carole turned away as Lisa moved forward. Stevie noticed that Judy and Max, too, kept their eyes averted. Stevie didn't even try to hear what her friend said to the dying horse. Lisa's voice murmured on for a minute or so, low but steady, and Stevie had the distinct feeling that her friend was trying to comfort Prancer as much as herself in those last seconds together.

Finally, though, the words stopped. Turning back toward Prancer, Stevie saw that Lisa was still holding the mare's head. But she was watching the vet calmly, her face dry and composed.

"We're ready, Judy," she said steadily.

Judy cleared her throat and nodded. Tears were visible in her own eyes as she checked her needle once more and then kneeled by Prancer's side. Stevie kept her gaze on the mare's face as Judy did her work. When the life faded from the horse's big, liquid brown eyes, Stevie knew that it was all over. Prancer was gone.

Stevie dropped to the straw beside Lisa and wrapped her arms around her. She felt Carole's arms encircling them both and was dimly aware that Judy had left the stall.

As the three friends cried together, Stevie couldn't help wondering why things had gone so horribly wrong for them—for Prancer, for her two best friends—on what was supposed to be a perfect day.

How are we ever going to recover from it all? Stevie wondered desolately, squeezing Lisa tighter than ever as sobs racked her body, and at the same time feeling the moisture from Carole's tears soaking the shoulder of her shirt. She glanced down at the still form of the mare resting on the straw beside them. *How are we going to recover?*

ABOUT THE AUTHOR

BONNIE BRYANT is the author of more than a hundred books about horses, including The Saddle Club series, Saddle Club Super Editions, and the Pony Tails series. She has also written novels and movie novelizations under her married name, B. B. Hiller.

Ms. Bryant began writing The Saddle Club in 1986. Although she had done some riding before that, she intensified her studies then and found herself learning right along with her characters Stevie, Carole, and Lisa. She claims that they are all much better riders than she is.

Ms. Bryant was born and raised in New York City. She still lives there, in Greenwich Village, with her two sons.